THE QUEST FOR THE
FUJI CIPHER

THE QUEST FOR THE FUJI CIPHER

A RICHARD HALLIBURTON ADVENTURE

BOOK 4

GARRETT DRAKE

The Quest for the Fuji Cipher
© Copyright 2020 Garrett Drake

First Edition 2020

Published in the United States of America

Green E-Books
PO Box 140654
Boise, ID 83714

For William Barstow,
a man dedicated to his craft
with a love for his students

"Just about a month from now I'm set adrift, with a diploma for a sail and lots of nerve for oars." — Richard Halliburton

CHAPTER 1

December 30, 1922
Vladivostok, Russia

RICHARD HALLIBURTON WRAPPED HIS FINGERS around the burly Russian's hand and eyed him closely from across the table. Nearly the entire crowd gathered at The Admiral's Pier pub had surrounded the two men. Another man stood looming over them and clasped his hands over theirs. Richard looked up at the self-appointed official for the arm wrestling match.

"Do you understand the rules?" the referee asked.

Richard nodded.

"This is your last chance to walk away from your match with Ivan and still retain your twenty dollars," the man said.

Richard forced a smile. "I suggest you let Ivan know this is his final opportunity to get out of this too."

The referee shrugged. "Since he's won over two hundred straight—"

"Three hundred," one patron corrected.

"Excuse me, three hundred straight," the referee said. "After so many wins that I've lost count, I doubt he feels threatened by you."

"Maybe someone should warn him," Richard said.

The patrons erupted with laughter.

"To the winner goes the spoils," the referee announced.

"Gentlemen, are you ready?"

Richard nodded, as did Ivan.

"Begin," the referee said as he released their hands and backed away from the table.

Richard gritted his teeth as he strained to keep his hand in an upright position. Sweat beaded on his forehead.

"Is that all you got?" Ivan said with a roar before chuckling.

How did I get myself into this mess?

Richard knew the answer, though he wished he'd ignored his impetuous spirit for once. But that was like telling a cow not to make milk, or Richard refusing an invitation to dance. Of course, Richard's penchant for dancing is what led him to this moment.

Anaya was the woman who urged Richard to get onto the dance floor. Now, she was sitting next to him, urging him on to victory.

"You can do it, Richard," she shouted. "Come on. Give it all you've got."

Richard's hand trembled as he struggled to maintain an upright position against the pressure Ivan applied. The Russian wasn't trembling and appeared to be breathing steadily, carrying on a conversation in broken English.

"Don't worry, Mr. American," Ivan said. "You won't be the first man from your country who lost to me."

Ivan smirked as he glared at Richard, who ignored the icy looks. Sensing imminent defeat, Richard placed his focus on his trembling hand and hoped to tire out Ivan.

"I-van, I-van, I-van, I-van," chanted the crowd. Others banged their mugs on the tables, heightening the tension.

"Don't give up," Anaya said. "He's starting to wear down. Keep going."

Richard wanted to believe her, but the reality was he'd

worn himself out just trying to stave off defeat. And he doubted he could muster enough strength to scratch out a victory. The only way he could avoid sinking into despair was to remember why he had agreed to this arm wrestling match, as ignoble of a cause as it was: to make a few quick bucks.

Before returning home, Richard had one last stop he wanted to make. Japan had long been a draw for him, particularly Mt. Fuji. But with Richard's funds practically depleted, his only chance to get on a ship bound for Japan from Vladivostok was to make a substantial sum of money and do it immediately. Anaya assured him it wouldn't be easy but it'd be worth it if he could pull the upset victory.

Once his knuckles made contact with the tabletop, Richard pushed aside the thought that he was about to be stranded in Siberia. And with only three inches of space separating his hand from the surface, his foolishness was going to cost him more than a return trip home. If he couldn't pull off a win, he would likely delay his dream of becoming an author, if not squelch it altogether. Getting stuck in Siberia wasn't going to impress the literary agent his handler Hank Foster promised to introduce him to upon returning to the United States.

"You've got him," Anaya screamed. "Do it now."

Richard growled as he strained to move Ivan's hand. But the Russian started to wane, ceding progress slowly.

By the time Richard forced their arms to a vertical position, his strength evaporated. He couldn't move his opponent's hand any farther. Moments later, he slammed Richard's hand onto the table. Like a judge pronouncing a ruling, the thud on the table trumpeted his loss.

The crowd broke into a cheer and started shouting the victor's name again.

"I-van, I-van, I-van, I-van."

The Russian wore a wide grin as he stood and pumped both fists in the air in rhythm with their chant. Then he snatched the money from the referee's hands and held it up, delighting his fans even more.

Mouth agape, Richard stared at the scene, unable to move. The sting of losing to a worthy foe didn't compare to squandering away the money he had in order to visit Japan.

"It's all right," Anaya said. "I'm sure you'll find a way to get where you want to go."

Richard sighed. "Maybe, but it just became more difficult."

He put on his coat and shuffled toward the door, unable to ignore the raucous cheers emanating from a bar-wide toast to Ivan.

"There might be another way," Anaya said as she walked alongside Richard.

He held the door open for her, gesturing for her to exit.

"Thank you," she said as they stepped outside. "Now, I'm not sure about this, but—"

Richard held up his hand and shook his head. "Let me stop you right there. I know that your intentions are to help me. But I listened to you and followed your advice and—"

"I warned you it would be risky."

"You did, but pardon me if I'm less inclined to hear your suggestion at the moment."

"I just want to help," she said, stroking her curly, golden locks.

"I appreciate the sentiment, but I need to figure out a way to do this on my own. Now, I do have one final possibility. If you would truly like to help me, please point me to the nearest station where I can send a telegram."

Anaya's face brightened with a wide smile. "A telegram? Is there some rich benefactor you've been shying away from asking?"

"If only that were true," he said with a chuckle. "No, I might be able to earn the money, though I would need an advance to cover my expenses for the journey."

"How exciting," she said as she clapped her hands.

Richard eyed her closely. "You do know this is a long shot, at least the part about getting someone to forward me the money."

"You needed about fifty dollars to complete your trip?" she asked.

"Approximately. If I had doubled my money, I wouldn't have hesitated to buy a ticket to Japan and figure out a way to raise the paltry sum of about five dollars. But as it stands, I only have five in my pocket. That certainly won't get me home. I'm going to have to stay here and work just to earn enough to purchase a ticket home now."

"That wouldn't be so bad now, would it?" she said with a wink.

"Wait a minute," he said. "This wasn't part of your ploy, was it?"

Anaya furrowed her brow. "Ploy? To do what?"

"Don't play coy with me," he said. "You want to keep me here, don't you?"

"You do flatter yourself a bit too much," she said. "It's not a becoming trait."

"Tell me I'm wrong."

"There's a telegraph station one block around that corner to the left," she said, pointing down the street. "Good luck, Mr. Halliburton."

She spun on her heels and marched off in the opposite direction.

Distraught over the prospect of staying in Vladivostok longer than anticipated, Richard hustled toward the telegraph station. Once he arrived, he cobbled together a note for his editor at *The Commercial Appeal* in Memphis.

> OPPORTUNITY TO WRITE STORY ON MT.
> FUJI. NEED $35 ADVANCE.

The message cost twenty-five cents to send. It'd take another twenty-five cents to receive the one returned, if one was at all. However, based on the last cable he received touting how popular his articles were with the newspaper's readership, Richard thought he'd at least get a reply, even if it was a rejection.

* * *

THE NEXT MORNING, Richard filled up on the breakfast served at his hostel. Skipping lunch wouldn't save much, but it all added up at this point. He hadn't finished his first cup of coffee before Anaya Lindstrom entered, waving an envelope at him.

"You won't believe what I have here," she said as she sat down at the opposite end of the table as Richard.

"Forty dollars and Ivan's admission of guilt that he cheated to beat me?" he asked.

"No, he beat you fairly. However, I was on my morning walk and passed the telegraph post I sent you to yesterday. And guess what? They have a message for you."

"Let me see that," he said, reaching for the paper.

She pulled it back out of his reach and wagged her finger at him. "I need you to promise to dance with me tonight."

Richard narrowed his eyes. "May I please have the envelope?"

"Promise?"

"Dancing with you brought me nothing but trouble. I don't know if I'm inclined to make the same mistake twice."

She shrugged. "Or you can sit on the dock and drink brandy by yourself."

"Given my current situation, that's sounding more appealing by the moment."

"Surely you jest."

Richard held out his hand again. "The envelope."

With a sigh, Anaya handed the document to him. "I'm hoping there's good news for you. What's it say?"

He read the words to himself: Want story on Mt. Fuji. Will pay $100 on receipt.

"Well?" Anaya asked. "Is there a reason to celebrate tonight?"

Richard shook his head. "I need to find a job so I can earn enough money to get home."

She grinned. "So you'll be staying?"

He took another sip of coffee. "Longer than I anticipated."

"I know you seem down about it, but you should cheer up. While you work, you can take advantage of this wonderful opportunity to explore Vladivostok more, not to mention be my exclusive dance partner."

"Look, I know this isn't your fault," Richard said. "I was the fool who heeded your advice and threw caution to the wind. But if there's one thing that will get me down, it's a missed opportunity. And not getting to see Japan before I go home is just that."

"I'm sure you'll have other chances."

Richard shrugged. "Perhaps, but if there's one thing I've learned while traveling the world, it's that nothing is for certain. The most thrilling moments in our lives are when we seize opportunity."

"Like arm wrestling a Russian lumberjack in Siberia?"

"Well, that will make for interesting fodder in a book,

but where did it get me? Not to Japan."

"But you had to try," she said. "And that spirit is what makes you a great adventurer. And who knows? Maybe I'll join you."

"From what I hear, there's not much dancing in Japan."

She stood. "Don't think you'll be able to get rid of me that easily. You're the one who's inspired me to see more of the world. I must be going now. I'll stop by and visit you later."

Richard finished his breakfast before heading out to send a telegraph to his father back home in Memphis.

> FUNDS DRIED UP. RETURNING HOME SOON.
> LOVE YOU.

Richard couldn't deny that he'd already experienced a lifetime of excitement with enough thrilling tales to share. But he felt disappointment too, knowing that one of his goals had been within reach but he couldn't touch it. He snatched up an abandoned newspaper and then strolled down to the docks to search for work.

After a short walk, he arrived at the water's edge and scanned the Golden Horn Bay. Ships packed with goods chugged around the bustling harbor of the Siberian port city. With his newspaper tucked away, Halliburton turned his attention to The Russian Empress. She was the only passenger vessel that sailed from Vladivostok to Japan with only one trip each week. Halliburton dug into his pocket and pulled out his remaining money to count it for the fifth time that morning. No matter how many times he looked, he couldn't magically make the funds transform into more.

He stradled the railing before opening his paper. He'd tried learning a few Russian words on his trip from China and had become proficient enough to get the gist of news articles.

The first he attempted to read was about the legalizing of an informal alliance forming the Union of Soviet Socialist Republics. The next one that grabbed his attention detailed the murder of a U.S. ambassador while on a boat traveling from China to Japan. After flipping through the section, he found a local story about an AEF soldier who'd stayed behind after U.S. troops pulled out of the region and established a successful restaurant.

A man eased up next to Halliburton, catching him off guard. He flinched as the man started speaking.

"Those things are . . . Sorry, I didn't mean to startle you."

"Nothing to worry about," Halliburton said as he spun around to face the man. "I just wasn't expecting anyone to speak to me. So, you were saying?"

"Newspapers are kind of boring when there isn't a war going on."

Halliburton shrugged. "I guess that depends on your perspective. Today's edition has news of an historic treaty, a murder at sea, and an American who's created a restaurant that is one of the most popular in Vladivostok."

"Well, that last story has my curiosity piqued," the man said before offering his hand to Halliburton. "George Linder, your friendly American restauranteur at your service."

Halliburton chuckled and looked at Linder before pointing at the paper. "You're him?"

He nodded. "In the flesh. I know that picture doesn't look too much like me, but that's because they wouldn't let me smile."

"I wish I could check out your establishment, but I'm in a little bit of a financial bind at the moment."

"What brings you here?"

Halliburton hopped down from his perch. "Adventure."

"You missed the boat on that one," Linder said with a chuckle. "If you'd been here about four years ago, you would've been in the thick of adventure, marching all across Siberia and fighting both enemies and the elements as part of the American Expeditionary Forces."

"Sounds exhilarating, yet opening a restaurant is a drastically different profession. What made you abandon the AEF and settle down to start a business?"

"Olga. When you find the one, you just know. You married?"

"In a manner of speaking."

Linder laughed. "And what does that mean?"

"My bride is adventure."

"Well, my friend, I hear you're looking for passage to Japan."

Richard cocked his head and eyed the man carefully. "And where did you hear this?"

Linder waved dismissively. "Doesn't matter. The point is I can help you get there."

"What's the catch?"

"None really. Just a favor you can do."

"And what kind of favor are we talking about?"

Linder gestured downtown. "Why don't you walk with me and I'll tell you all about it?"

CHAPTER 2

AS A LIGHT SNOW BEGAN TO FALL, RICHARD HUSTLED after Linder as he twirled his cane and broke into a torrid pace. If he had a limp, Richard didn't notice. He surmised that Linder's stick topped with a brass globe was either for show or the business end of a stealthy weapon.

"Where are we going?" Richard asked once he caught up.

"You'll see. Just try to keep up."

Linder didn't break his stride when two young boys darted in front of him while throwing snowballs at each other.

"How did you know my name?" Richard asked.

"Your reputation precedes you."

"I have a reputation here?"

Linder didn't say anything as he approached the intersection. Instead of crossing the street, he took a hard right, and that's when Richard saw it: the American consulate.

"Who told you about me?" Richard asked.

"I'll answer all your questions just as soon as we get inside," Linder said, nodding at the building. "They're waiting for you."

Richard stopped. "Waiting for me?"

Linder continued walking toward the front steps. "That's what I said. Now, hurry along. We don't want to keep anyone waiting."

Richard sighed and resisted the urge to follow Linder. "I appreciate the brisk walk, but I'm going back to the docks."

Linder spun on his heels and marched toward Richard. "Did you miss the part where I said they're waiting for you?"

Richard didn't flinch. "You said you'd tell me all about it while we walked. But I see where we're going, and I'm not interested. I've done enough for the government on this trip. Now, it's time for those people who co-opted me into working for them to uphold their end of the bargain before I do anything else."

Linder eyed Richard closely. "I thought you wanted to go to Japan."

"Not that badly."

"Would you at least hear them out?"

Richard shook his head. "Not without hearing from you first."

"Oh, come on, Mr. Halliburton. Won't you be a reasonable man and at least listen to their proposal?"

Richard held his ground. "What do you do for them?"

"I'm more or less retired, but on occasion they deploy me to help out."

"And by helping out in this case, you mean dragging me into the consulate, don't you?"

"Look, come or don't come. It makes no difference to me. I just know there's an important mission that requires someone with your particular skill set."

"And what exactly is that?"

Linder clasped his hands behind his back and started to pace around Richard, eyeing him closely. "I was told that you're very slippery, hard to catch, and even more challenging to trap in a story. Those are both well-honed instincts."

"I wouldn't call them instinctual," Richard said. "More like necessary to survive. How much have you traveled around Africa and Asia, Mr. Linder?"

"Enough to understand exactly what you're talking about. And that is why your government needs you for this trip."

Richard glanced at the consulate building. "I wouldn't be so arrogant as to assume that I was the first choice."

"And you'd be right."

"What happened to the first agent?"

"An unfortunate accident," Linder said. "He broke his leg a few hours before he was scheduled to proceed with the assignment."

"In that case, I'll listen," Richard said. "But I'm not making any promises."

"Excellent," Linder said as he turned around and gestured toward the building. "Shall we?"

Richard remained a half-step behind Linder. As they entered, a pair of women greeted the two men. After a brief conversation, one of the women ushered the duo down a hallway and into a room where three men sat at one end of a conference room table. They all rose, introducing themselves as they offered their hands.

"Mr. Halliburton," the first man said, "it is a great honor to finally meet you. After reading about your exploits in Egypt, India, and China, I feel like I know you already. John Evans, Army Intelligence."

The other two Army officers, Paul Collier and Lee Maxwell, flanked Evans and introduced themselves.

"Where exactly did you read about my exploits?" Richard asked.

"I spoke with Hank Foster yesterday about you," Evans said. "You come very highly recommended."

Richard stroked his chin as he surveyed the men at the table. "While flattery might be able to lure me onto a dance floor, it's not going to work when it comes to a perilous mission."

"From what I understand, danger is your middle name," Evans said. "Foster told me that you run into the fray, not from it."

"I've been known to do that on occasion, but only when the situation calls for it. And since Mr. Linder here has been rather tight-lipped about this mission, I'm not sure this request meets that high standard."

"I can assure you it does," Maxwell said.

Richard leaned forward, hands clasped in front of him. "I'm afraid I'll need more than your verbal assurances."

Evans opened a file before sliding it across the table to Richard. "Everything you need to know about this operation is right there. We captured a Japanese cipher used to decrypt messages passed between field agents and the military leaders at their command center. The officer who captured this device is unable to make the long journey and hand deliver it to our embassy in Japan."

"Sounds simple enough," Richard said. "Are you sure you need me to do this?"

Evans pulled the file back. "We need someone who the Japanese won't suspect."

Richard scanned the men's faces. "What exactly happened to the first courier?"

"Broke his leg," Evans said.

"In an automobile accident," Maxwell added.

"And he couldn't deliver it with a broken leg?" Richard asked. "Sitting down on a ship for a short voyage and then riding in a train doesn't exactly require two working legs. Are you telling me the truth?"

"Yes," Evans said.

Richard furrowed his brow. "The whole truth?"

"Well . . ." Evans sucked a breath through his teeth, "there may be one other detail we omitted."

"Out with it," Richard said, narrowing his eyes.

"The previous agent also suffered some other injuries," Evans said.

Richard held out his hand in a gesture for Evans to continue. "Such as?"

"Death," Maxwell said. "The agent died in the accident."

"It wasn't an accident, was it?" Richard asked.

"Another Japanese spy caught our man and killed him a few hours after he'd obtained possession of the cipher. However, the first thing he did was make a duplicate of the cipher, which we recovered from his hotel room."

Richard stood and backed away from the table. "Thank you for the opportunity, gentlemen, but I'll pass on this one."

"Oh, come on," Evans said. "That doesn't sound like the Richard Halliburton from Foster's reports about you."

"The nature of Foster's assignments were mostly intelligence gathering," Richard said. "On occasion, I may have fought against armed Germans to ensure that they didn't abscond with millions of dollars in treasure back to their motherland. But I have run up against the Japanese, and they are on a whole different level. They're more skilled and far more ruthless."

"But no one will know you have the cipher," Evans said. "Think of this as an all-expenses-paid trip to Japan simply for delivering a small package. It'll probably be the least dangerous task you've performed for Army Intelligence."

"Is that what you told the previous agent?" Richard asked.

"That was a different situation," Evans said. "The Japanese don't even know we have another cipher in our possession—and for your sake, it's best we keep it that way."

"I'm sorry, but I won't change my mind," Richard said. "I'm sure you can find someone else to handle the assignment if it's truly that simple, though I suspect you're overselling the ease at which this cipher could be delivered. Good luck."

Evans sighed and shook his head. "We might be able to find someone, but it'll be too late. Pertinent messages of utmost importance are being sent back and forth each day between Japanese spies and their military. The speed at which we intercept these communiques and interpret them might be the difference in thwarting an attack. In short, each day we delay in getting this device to our people in Tokyo could possibly cost hundreds, if not thousands, of lives."

"You've made a compelling pitch," Richard said, "but it hasn't moved me. This is a simple assignment. I'm disappointed I can't go to Japan, but it can wait. I will return. And I'm confident you'll be able to lure someone else into such a task, if it's really as simple and benign as you say. Good day, gentlemen."

Richard spun and headed toward the door.

"Let me know if you change your mind," Evans said.

Richard didn't turn around, acknowledging the comment only by waving his hand in the air as he strode into the hallway.

He suffered other injuries, such as death.

Richard shook his head as he recalled the conversation.

"I love adventure, but even I have my limits," he muttered to himself.

Failing to view Mt. Fuji in person was disappointing, but he was certain there'd be other opportunities, the kind he'd get on his own terms instead of being the military's glorified errand boy.

With that issue settled, Halliburton decided he needed to find a job if he intended to ever eat again, much less return home.

CHAPTER 3

RICHARD VENTURED INTO ONE SHOP AFTER ANOTHER, searching for anyone willing to hire him. The first two businesses he entered weren't owned by men who spoke any English. When he reached the third business, the man managing the store told him that his boss only hired locals. And while Richard normally embraced such a challenge, the longing to see his family in Memphis started to outweigh any desire he had for adventure, whether compelled or by his own choice.

After the twelfth rejection, Richard shuffled outside before taking a seat on the icy steps. He glanced skyward and watched a sheet of snow descend around him. In a matter of minutes, Vladivostok had a fresh blanket of powder.

"Isn't it just wonderful?" asked a woman.

Richard nodded subtly before he recognized the voice. He glanced up at her and sighed.

"I don't have any more money for arm wrestling or anything else, to be quite frank," he said as he eyed Anaya closely.

She sat next to him and then put her hand on his knee. "I'm so sorry about all that, really, I am. So, I've been thinking about how I could make it up to you."

Richard waved dismissively. "You've done more than enough already."

"And then a thought occurred to me," she said, ignoring his comment and continuing. "I could help Mr. Halliburton get home."

"Don't bother yourself with this affair," Richard said. "It's not necessary and—"

"So I pondered how I might be able to secure you a seat on the next boat bound for the United States, and I realized just how simple it would be for me to—"

"Please, Anaya," Richard said, grabbing Anaya's wrist and removing her hand from his leg. "I don't need your help."

She drew back and eyed him closely. "So you've found another way?"

"Not yet," he said as he kicked at the snow with the toe of his boot. "But I'll figure out something."

"Since you're so creative, I guess you don't want to hear what I have to say then."

Richard sighed. He wasn't as upset with Anaya as he was with himself. While she was trying to help him by suggesting a quick way to make some money, Richard could only blame himself—and he knew it.

"Look, I'm sorry," Richard said, his gaze still focused on the ground. "I knew better than to try some stunt like that, and I've taken it out on you. I've been gone from Memphis for a while now, and I just want to get back home."

"What about Japan?"

"I'm sure I'll get another opportunity."

"In that case, you'll definitely want to hear what I have to say."

Richard looked up and shrugged. "Go ahead. It's not like I'm going to lose any more money from listening to one of your ideas."

"I forgot to mention to you an important piece of information," she said.

"And what's that?"

"My uncle owns several shipping lines, including a passenger vessel that embarks for San Francisco every two weeks."

Richard's mouth fell agape. "Otto Lindstrom is your uncle? The Otto Lindstrom?"

"That's the one."

"And you never thought to mention this to me before suggesting that I wrestle that Russian lumberjack?"

Anaya shrugged. "I thought you wanted to go to Japan, but he doesn't have any passenger ships that go there."

"But cargo ships?"

"On occasion, but his focus is on managing the trade business with Europe and India along with some new opportunities opening up in the United States."

"I could earn my keep by serving as a deckhand," Richard said. "I've become quite adept at working on various types of vessels since I left home."

"I'm sorry," she said. "I didn't think of that before as an option for you. My uncle's ships might go to Japan once a month or so, and I knew you wanted to go right away."

"My impatience will likely be the death of me," he said. "And you're right. I don't have the time or the money to wait for something like that. But a voyage back home? When does the next ship leave?"

"There's one that leaves tomorrow for San Francisco," she said. "I told my uncle about you, and he said that if you could do something to pay your way, he'd allow you on board. So, do you have any special skills that would satisfy his demand?"

"Do his ships have orchestras?"

"I believe they do."

"I can play the violin," Richard said. "I'm not going to

win first chair in any symphony, but my ability is more than adequate."

"Very well then," she said. "I'll let him know. I'm sure that will be sufficient. Start packing, and I'll be back with all the details."

"Thank you," Richard said. "And I'm really sorry about earlier."

"Think nothing of it," she said. "Maybe you can work off your penance by dancing with me tonight before you leave."

"Is that really a punishment?" he asked with a wry grin.

"Not for you," she said. "But if you don't like that idea, I can always arrange for a rematch with the lumberjack."

"Dancing will be just fine," he said.

"Great," she said. "I'll meet you at the Admiral's Pier at seven o'clock. And I'll have your boarding pass with me. Don't be late."

"I wouldn't dream of it."

Richard watched Anaya hustle away, her footsteps crunching in the fresh snow. Once she disappeared around the corner, he took a deep breath and exhaled. While he found Vladivostok interesting, he wasn't keen on the idea of spending any more time in the port city than he had to. However, Richard wasn't going to complain about how the past couple of years abroad had gone. He'd experienced a lifetime of adventure already, but he did miss his parents— and the smell of their kitchen after his mother pulled out a pan of piping hot biscuits.

Without the need to search for work, Richard returned to his hostel to pack up his things. After he shoved the last of his belongings into his bag, he heard a knock on the door. He strode over to it and asked who it was.

"An old friend," the man said.

Richard recognized the voice, but he wasn't sure he was prepared for the ensuing conversation. Once the door swung open, Richard confirmed the identity of his visitor.

Draped in a thick, brown coat, Hank Foster held his hat in his hand as he stood in front of Richard's door.

"What a surprise, Hank," Richard said, forcing a smile. "What brings you to Siberia?"

"This isn't a conversation I want to have in the hall," Foster said.

"By all means, come in," Richard said, waving Foster into the room. "She's not much, but she will at least afford us some privacy."

"Thank you," Foster said as he eased inside.

Richard pulled the door shut behind his guest.

"You don't really look surprised to see me," Foster said as he sat down in a chair in one corner of the room.

Richard settled onto the foot of the bed. "I'm not, though I am shocked at the speed in which you arrived. Based on my conversation with Evans at the consulate yesterday, I figured it was only a matter of time."

"And you appear to be planning to leave very soon, too."

Richard nodded. "That's what I hope to do, though you know what people say about men's best laid plans, right?"

"They often go awry," Foster said with a hint of a smile. "Robert Burns—he's my favorite Scottish poet."

"If you're here to convince me to change my mind, I wish you well in your fruitless endeavor," Richard said. "You'll find that I'm quite stubborn when I've finally decided to do something."

"Such as going to Japan and climbing Mt. Fuji?" Foster asked.

"Those are still very much my plans, just not any time in the near future. I miss my family and—"

"Is that what you're telling yourself, Richard? That you're going to come back one day to this part of the world and climb up Mt. Fuji? Because you sure as hell aren't doing it now in the dead of winter."

"Now you're just trying to goad me into it," Richard said. "But it won't work. I've already secured a way home. I need a break from all your harrowing assignments."

Foster chuckled and shook his head. "Now if I believed that, I would also be purchasing some ocean front property in Nebraska. So, really, Richard, what's her name?"

Richard cocked his head to one side and furrowed his brow. "Her name?"

"Yeah, the broad you're just itching to see. What's her name?"

"There isn't a woman."

Foster waved dismissively. "I don't believe that. There's always a woman."

"Well, I guess there is one."

"Ah, ha. I knew it. Who is she? What makes her so special that you're willing to put an opportunity for adventure on hold with no guarantees that you'll ever be back in this part of the world?"

"Her name is Nelle Halliburton, and she makes the best damn biscuits you'll ever put in your mouth."

"Oh, for goodness sake. You're homesick? Is that what this is about?"

Richard shrugged. "I'm tired, Hank. I need a break. Chasing down the Reichswehr and every other sinister group operating in Africa and Asia has left me worn out. Besides, I still want to write."

"And you will," Foster said. "But I really need you to do this for me. You have no idea how important this mission is. And you're the only one qualified to get it done in a timely manner."

"Look, I've done plenty for you. Just get me the contact information for the publisher you told me about and let's call it good."

Foster sighed. "Are you sure I can't convince you otherwise?"

Richard shook his head. "I've made up my mind. I'm going home, but I will be back."

"Fine, I'll meet you at the docks in the morning with the information for the publisher. You'll be a world famous author before you know it, that much I'm sure of."

"I appreciate the opportunities you gave me. And maybe I'll help you out again in the future."

"I won't say no to that," Foster said as he put his hat on. "Good luck, Richard. See you in the morning."

Richard shut the door behind Foster and then collapsed onto the bed. The conversation had been draining as well as difficult. Saying no to Foster wasn't easy, but Richard resisted the urge. Another chapter in his life was just in reach, and he couldn't wait to dive into it.

* * *

WHEN RICHARD APPROACHED The Admiral's Pier at the stroke of 7:00 p.m., he noticed a line of people struggling to get inside. A pair of bearded men with bulging muscles fought to keep the throng outside. Richard walked up to what seemed like the back of the line to inquire about what was happening.

Closer to the front, the throng continued to press against the bouncers while chanting something in Russian. As Richard surveyed the situation, he wondered how he was going to find Anaya to get his boarding pass.

Before doing anything rash, he felt a tap on his shoulder. He spun around to find Anaya standing before him and wearing a wide grin.

"What's this all about?" Richard asked, glancing back toward the pub. "You didn't promise anyone that I would be wrestling that blockhead again, did you?"

She laughed. "No, of course, not. But they are here to see you."

"Me?" Richard asked as he drew back. "What on Earth for? Surely you're joking?"

"It's a tradition that The Royal Utö orchestra plays at The Admiral's Pier the night before leaving port," she said. "And, so, you're up."

"Wait a minute," he said. "I'm supposed to play? Right now?"

"My uncle wanted to hear you play before he gave you free passage."

Richard eyed her closely. "So, this is an audition of sorts?"

"Not of sorts. It is a true audition. If you meet my uncle's standards, you'll receive your boarding pass."

"And if not?"

"You'll have to earn enough money to purchase a ticket like everyone else."

"You've got to be joking," he said.

"No, I'm not. But why do you seem so concerned? You weren't lying to me about your ability to play the violin, were you?"

"I can play it, but I get extremely nervous in front of a large crowd of people."

"Then you better get over it—and fast."

"I haven't even had a chance to practice or warm up."

Anaya shoved Richard in the back, directing him around the corner of the building.

"Where are we going?" he asked.

"The only way we're getting inside," she said.

She hustled past and ushered him through the back entrance. Moments later, Richard was handed a violin along with several pieces of sheet music. He settled into his seat along with a dozen other musicians.

"Ready?" the man seated next to Richard asked.

Richard wanted to shake his head, but he couldn't. He fingered the strings on the fret and raised his bow. Before he knew it, he was sawing away along with the rest of the makeshift orchestra.

Richard swallowed hard after the first song when he looked up at the applauding crowd. Before he had an opportunity to revel in the moment, the conductor nodded at the rest of the musicians and started in on the next song, a truncated version of Tchaikovsky's 1812 Overture. Richard was familiar with the piece and had no problems handling the tender introduction that relied upon the strings to carry the tune.

Three more songs later, Richard finished playing and rubbed the tips of his fingers in an attempt to soothe them. With his calluses long gone, the searing pain made him wonder if he could sustain playing every night for the two-week trip across the Pacific Ocean. He was still looking down at his hands when he felt a slap on the back. Richard looked up to see Otto Lindstrom, arguably one of the most powerful men in this part of the world. Lindstrom's shipping enterprise had blossomed, enabling him to become one of the titans of the industry.

"That was outstanding playing, lad," Lindstrom said.

Richard stood and shook Lindstrom's hand. "Thank you, sir. I didn't realize I'd be thrown into the fire like that, but I'm glad it sounded sufficient."

"Sufficient?" Lindstrom said with a chuckle. "My boy, you're far too modest. That was truly amazing, especially for what we're used to around here."

"You're too kind," Richard said.

"I've been called worse," Lindstrom said as he whipped out a boarding pass and then handed it to Richard. "Enjoy your trip."

"Thank you, sir. I—"

Richard didn't even finish expressing his gratitude before Lindstrom spun and walked away into an adoring audience. He glad-handed every one that wanted to speak to him before being swallowed up by the crowd.

Anaya bounded up to Richard. "What do you think? Isn't he a gentleman in every sense of the word? I absolutely adore him."

"He's more than gracious for letting me on this voyage."

"You're going to earn your way, but I can't say I remember seeing Uncle Otto glow like that. I don't think you have any idea how much he enjoyed your addition to the orchestra."

"Well, I must get back. I have a long journey ahead."

Anaya stuck her bottom lip out and batted her crystal-blue eyes at him. "But you said we were going to dance."

"Oh, all right," he said. "Just one dance. After that, I have to go."

* * *

WHEN RICHARD AWOKE, he scrambled to his feet and checked the clock: 6:45 a.m. After snatching his bag, Richard raced out of the hostel and down to the ship, which was nearly finished. He flashed his boarding pass to the man on the dock, who waved Richard onboard. However, he didn't get any farther than onboard when someone shuffled in front of him and impeded his path up the ramp and onto the ship.

"Excuse me, sir," Richard said with his head down as he attempted to push his way past the man.

The man didn't budge, instead putting a shoulder into

Richard's chest.

"Sir, I—" Richard said before looking up and coming face to face with Hank Foster.

"Richard," Foster said.

"No, no, no. I already gave you my decision. Now, please step aside so I can get on board. I'm actually part of the staff."

"Is that how you want this voyage to be? You dwelling far below deck, sleeping on an uncomfortable bed made even more uncomfortable by the tempests that stir in the Pacific?"

"What part of no don't you understand? It's really a simple answer."

"Don't make me beg, Richard."

Richard smiled wryly. "Never considered that, but that would be some quality entertainment. Perhaps you can join us on the trip, and when the orchestra isn't playing you can provide us with a sideshow to enthrall the masses where you ask me a hundred different ways to do something for you. And every time I reject you. The audience will be expecting me to accept your offer at any moment, but I'm set in my ways, creating a tension-filled story."

"I'd rather—"

"What?" Richard asked. "You'd rather what?"

Foster huffed. "Just don't get on this ship, please. I need you. Your government needs you."

"I'm going home, okay? Now, please step aside and let me pass."

Foster moved back and gestured for Richard to pass.

"Thank you," Richard said as he flung his bag over his shoulder and strode past Foster.

"Good luck, Richard," Foster said. "I'm really disappointed, especially after I received a telegram this morning from my friend at the Feakins Agency."

Richard stopped and slowly turned around. "I thought

we had a deal. I help you out and then you help me connect with your publisher, not a speaking agent."

"We did," Foster said, dangling the note in front of Richard, "but your potential agent is very interested in material on Japan. It's something his speakers don't have much of. And without it, I'm not sure he'll be willing to take you on."

Richard snatched up the letter, scanning it quickly. "How do I even know this is real?"

"Feel free to contact him when you get back to the United States."

"This feels like extortion."

"Look, I'm just passing along the message. It's something you wanted to do a few days ago. And now you can. All it includes is a short little errand for Uncle Sam. You can kill two birds with one stone."

"It's more like two stones to kill one bird."

"However you want to look at it, that's your prerogative. But you have a decision to make—and I don't think you're really left with much of a choice if you want that publishing deal."

Richard sighed, stewing for a moment as he stared out across the water. The whole note could've been concocted by Foster, which Richard wouldn't put past the Army Intelligence officer. But if the publisher actually sent that note, Richard stood to lose the chance of a lifetime.

"Fine," he said. "I'll do it. But I'm not exactly thrilled to be working for any publisher that treats a prospective author this way."

"Welcome to the world of publishing," Foster said. "It's almost as seedy as the world of espionage."

"And lucky me," Richard said. "I've got a foot in each one of them."

"Well, let's get going. Your next adventure awaits."

CHAPTER 4

RICHARD LUGGED THE TWO SACKS OF MAIL ALONG with his bag onto The Ardent, an aging steamship that made a weekly trip between Vladivostok, Russia and Tsuruga, Japan. For the past three days, he'd spent his time at the consulate going over all the details of his delivery and learning a few basic phrases in Japanese. The Ardent was scheduled to depart several days earlier, but the icy waters in the Sea of Japan had other plans. With the delay, Richard had the extra time he needed to prepare for his trip and subsequent mission.

After Richard handed his boarding pass to the attendant at the dock, the man stamped the document and directed Richard to the bowels of the boat. Upon arriving in his room, he shook his head, wondering if there was a mistake. He flagged down a porter to let him inspect the piece of paper.

"This is your room," the man said, nodding at Richard's assigned door. "It's correct."

"Down here," Richard said. "It's dank and dark."

"You should've paid for a first class ticket," the man said with a shrug before scurrying away.

Richard agreed, though Foster had apologized when handing over the third-class ticket. According to him, all the other cabins were full.

It's just for two nights. I suppose I can manage.

Resigned to his fate, Richard flung his bag onto the floor and placed the two mail sacks in the closet. He plopped down on the bed to test it out. Seconds later, he sprang to his feet and stared back at it.

I'll never get any sleep on that thing.

The mattress hardly had any springs left in it, and what remained felt like rocks. Richard hopped up and decided to explore the steamship, anything to get out of his musty room.

Unlike the vessel he'd taken from the U.S. to Europe, this one was low on amenities. Aside from the activities in first class, the rest of the decks were akin to cattle herding. Passengers were let out to eat, allowed to spend some time roaming around a small area, and then directed back into their rooms at night.

The minutes seemed to drip by. Richard passed the time by reading A Study in Scarlet by Sir Arthur Conan Doyle he'd found among the sparse offerings in the ship's library. After dinner, he read a few chapters before eventually falling asleep.

When Richard awoke the next morning, he could hardly move, his back stiff from the ill-suited bed. He groaned as he sat up and then staggered over to his bag to get a fresh set of clothes. Looking at his watch, he grimaced, knowing he still had at least another thirty-six hours before they reached port in Tsuruga.

He spent most of his day reading, finishing up Doyle's book and falling in love with the character of Sherlock Holmes. When dinnertime arrived, Richard shuffled into the hallway and proceeded to lock the door to his room, securing the mail with the cipher tucked safely inside the pouches. He turned to head down the corridor to go to eat but froze when a young woman approached him. She wore a red dress with a printed pattern of cherry blossoms, her dark hair pulled up in a taut bun.

"Excuse me, are you going to dinner now?" she asked in English.

Richard nodded. "Do you need an escort to dinner?"

"That would be most appreciated."

"Richard Halliburton, at your service, ma'am," he said.

"My name is Hisako, and it's a pleasure to meet you."

He offered her his arm and ushered her to the dining room. Over the meal, they exchanged stories about adventures in traveling as well as what their homelands were like.

"Tell me about Mt. Fuji," Richard said. "I want to climb it."

"You'll have to wait for that," she said. "No guide will take you to the summit until the weather warms up. It's treacherous to make such an attempt in the winter, so much so that it's never been done."

"That sounds like a challenge."

Hisako shook her head. "No, that's a warning. Don't dare try that—at least, not if you value your life. The weather can change up there in a matter of minutes."

"I'm always up for a little excitement."

"Not that kind," she said. "You don't want anything to do with Mt. Fuji during this season."

As dinner progressed, Richard learned that Hisako was returning from Russia where she'd gone to perform a dance at a cultural festival in Moscow. She'd been all over the world as part of a small troop that represented Japan internationally. However, she'd yet to visit the United States, a fact she expressed disappointment over.

"I hear America is really beautiful," she said. "One day, I hope I'll get the chance to visit there, maybe even dance for your president."

"President Harding? He'd probably like that."

"Of course he would."

"No, Harding would especially like that, if you know what I mean."

"I'm not sure I do," she said before dabbing the corners of her mouth with her napkin.

Richard glanced around the room before he leaned close, speaking in a hushed tone. "It's just a rumor at this point, but the president has quite the reputation as being a little sweet on the ladies, the kind his wife wouldn't approve of."

"I understand," she said. "Sounds like most world leaders, if I must be frank."

After dinner concluded, Hisako looked at Richard. "Any plans for this evening?"

"I haven't considered anything other than trying to find another book to read in the library."

"A dashing young man like yourself isn't going to dance?"

"I love to dance, but not after last night's sleep."

"What happened?"

"My lumpy bed feels as if it's stuffed with rocks. When I woke up, I thought someone had beaten me in the back with a chef's mallet. As a result of that, I'm ever so sore. And if you know me, you'd understand how awful I must feel, for dancing is one of my greatest joys."

Hisako smiled and patted Richard on his hand. "Dancing will help you limber up."

"I'm not sure I believe that."

"There's only one way to find out. Come, join me."

Richard rubbed the lower part of his back and grimaced. "I don't know."

"Don't be a stick in the mud. It'll be fun."

"Oh, all right," Richard said with a sigh before he trudged off with Hisako to the dance floor.

The community hall was half full as the ship's orchestra had just begun their first set. Richard led Hisako onto the floor to dance where they started with the Fox Trot to Irving Berlin's "Say It with Music." After a few minutes, Richard's back started to loosen up. However, three songs later, searing pain returned—and stronger than before.

"I'm sorry," Richard said. "I just can't do this anymore. Let me be a gentleman and walk you back to your room."

"If you insist," Hisako said.

The two chatted about dancing as they walked down the corridor leading to their quarters. When they arrived outside Hisako's door, she took his hands in hers.

"Thank you for making the effort tonight, even though I can tell you're in quite a bit of pain."

"I appreciate you giving me a push," he said before wincing.

"If you'd allow me to, I could give you a massage. Maybe it'd help you get a better night of sleep."

"That's a kind offer, but I think I'm just going back to my room. I'm definitely not like President Harding."

Hisako blushed. "Oh, no. That's not why I was asking. I'm trained in Anma, an ancient Japanese massage technique. You'd be surprised how much it might help."

"I don't want to be any trouble."

"You won't be. Please, come in."

"All right," Richard said. "If you insist."

"I do."

Richard entered her room and shuffled to one side of the tight quarters as he waited for Hisako. She squeezed past him before gesturing for him to sit down on her bed.

"Mine is not made of rocks," she said with a soft laugh.

Richard settled onto the firm mattress before wondering how he was assigned the cabin with most likely the worst bed on the entire ship.

"Before we begin, Anma is about teaching your body to relax. And that process starts with a cup of tea. I will go down the hall to get us some and be right back."

Richard glanced around the stark room, which was identical to his with the exception of the more comfortable bed. Hanging up in the small closet were a pair of pink and purple kimonos decorated with flowery images. A picture of Hisako and a man dressed in military attire sat on her nightstand.

She returned a couple minutes later with a pair of mugs. "Here you go," she said. "Herbal tea from my country."

"It smells delicious," Richard said as he took the teacup from her. Then he glanced at her photograph. "Is that your fiancé?"

"One day soon, I hope," she said. "He's made me plenty of promises before, but I can never be sure if he's going to keep his word."

"Well, he'd be a fool if he passed up a kind-hearted soul like yourself."

Hisako's face reddened before she put her head down, hiding behind her cup.

"I didn't mean to embarrass you," he said.

"It's all right," she said. "It's not the sort of thing I'm used to talking about with strangers."

Once Richard finished his tea, Hisako instructed him to lie down on his back. Upon following her instructions, Richard felt at ease for the first time since he'd set foot on the ship. He closed his eyes. And in a matter of seconds, he was sound asleep.

* * *

THE POUNDING on the door awoke Richard from his slumber. With no portal to view the sea, he had no idea what time it was. And initially, he'd forgotten where he was or what he was doing there. Then everything came back to him. He was in Hisako's room getting a massage and . . .

The picture is gone. And so are her dresses.

"Please open up," a man said tersely. "It's past time to exit."

Richard sat up and rubbed his face. Then he glanced at his watch.

Two o'clock. How on Earth did I—

Richard scrambled to his feet and shot down the hallway to his room, brushing up against the porter as he went. The door was wide open, and his belongings were piled in the middle of the floor.

"Where is everyone?" Richard shouted.

"They've left, like they're supposed to," the porter said.

"But I—"

"That wasn't your room, was it?"

"No, this is my room," Richard said as he staggered back out into the hallway, his head aching. "I don't know what happened. The last thing I remember, I was drinking some tea and then—"

The porter shook his head. "I wasn't there, lad. I have no idea what happened to you. But I know what better happen if you don't want to return to Vladivostok and pay a handsome price when we arrive."

"Okay, okay," Richard said. "I'm going."

He ran back into his room as he considered the possibilities. Then his heart started pounding.

The cipher!

He dug his hand into the mail pouch where he'd hidden it—but the device was gone.

CHAPTER 5

January 3, 1923
Tsuruga, Japan

RICHARD SLUNG THE TWO POSTAL SACKS AND HIS BAG over his shoulder before hustling through *The Ardent* in search of anyone who could help him. Most of the ship's staff had already begun cleaning the interior in preparation for the next voyagers set to board later that afternoon. And everyone Richard stopped seemed either disinterested in helping or unable to speak English. He stomped his foot and cursed under his breath.

"Is there something I can help you with?" a porter asked Richard.

"Finally, yes! As a matter of fact, there is."

"Out with it, young man."

"I'm looking for a Japanese woman about this tall with straight, dark hair. She was wearing a red dress with a colorful flower print," Richard said.

The man chuckled and put his arm around Richard's shoulder. "Look around you. You've just landed in Japan. This entire island is literally full of women who look just like the one you described. Good luck."

Richard dropped everything at his feet as he scanned the docks and walkways surrounding the boat. Against the backdrop of the frosted Ryohaku mountains, scores of women shuffled along wearing coats to combat the frigid temperatures, their faces shrouded by fur-lined hoods.

"I'll never be able to find her now," he said aloud.

The man smiled and then whistled as he walked away.

Richard picked up his bags and trudged down the ramp of the ship to a customs line. Most of the passengers had long since departed, but a few stragglers remained, haggling with agents over what they could bring into the country.

As he approached an official for processing, Richard held up the mail pouches, displaying the U.S. Mail stamp on the side. The man's eyes widened as he gestured for one of the guards to attend to Richard. Seconds later, security personnel swarmed around him, barking orders in broken English.

Confused by the scene, Richard set down the bags and lifted his hands in the air in a gesture of surrender. "I'm just making a delivery."

"Come with us," one guard ordered.

Richard followed the men into a wooden office constructed on the docks. Inside, an elderly man sat behind a desk and stroked his long white beard that tickled the paper in front of him. He puffed on a pipe and eyed Richard closely.

"What is your name?" the apparent man in charged asked.

"Richard Halliburton, sir. I don't mean any harm, honest. I'm just here to—"

"Silence," the man said, raising his flattened right palm in the air. "I only want you to answer my questions. Understand?"

Richard nodded. He found the situation more and more unsettling with the introduction of each new authority figure, keeping him from enjoying the majestic scenery outside. This wasn't how he imagined entering Japan, or any other country for that matter. He wanted to revel in the intoxicating moment of venturing into a new land where an intriguing culture collided with a storied history. But instead, he wondered if this experience was going to be Gibraltar all over again where he spent a few nights in prison. Based on the stern expression on the faces of the men huddled together around their boss, Richard thought a few nights in jail might make him feel as if he'd escaped a harsher punishment.

"What brings you to Tsuruga?" the man asked.

"I want to see Japan, sir," Richard said. "And some gentlemen at the U.S. consulate in Vladivostok asked me to deliver these mailbags to the consulate in Tokyo. Nothing more, nothing less."

"We'll need to inspect your mail."

"I understand," Richard said. "I'm confident you'll find everything in lawful order."

"That's for me to decide, not you."

"Of course," Richard said as he gestured toward the bags. "Feel free to search everything."

"We will."

A pair of guards who were standing against the wall rushed over to Richard and escorted him to an adjacent room. He sat down on a bench and stared out the window at The Ardent. The steamship appeared undisturbed, the waves lapping against the docks as workers continued to prepare the vessel. He saw a woman hustling up the ramp to enter the boat who looked like Hisako. Richard stood and attempted to get a closer look through the window when he was met with a firm fist to his chest.

"Sit," the man said.

"But I think that woman—"

"Sit," he said, pointing back at the seat.

Richard sighed and sat down, unsure if he'd seen Hisako or not. He was far enough away that he couldn't determine anything definitively. But if it was, he had plenty of questions for her.

A half-hour later, the official overseeing the customs entered the room.

"Am I free to go now?" Richard asked.

"We received a telegram yesterday informing us of your arrival and the request to grant you passage to Tokyo," the man said. "We're going to permit you to travel to Tokyo, but not alone."

"Pardon me, but I thought—"

The man held up his hand before a rotund man with his dark hair arranged in a bun on the top of his head strode into the room. "This is Hideki Yutaka. He will be accompanying you on your journey. Where you go, he goes. Understood?"

Richard nodded and then sighed. He didn't find the prospect appealing, but there didn't appear much else he could do about it.

"Can I have my bags back?" Richard asked.

Yutaka dropped them at Richard's feet, along with his luggage. "Lead the way."

* * *

RICHARD LUGGED the mail sacks into the train bound for Tokyo. He glanced over his shoulder to watch Yutaka climbing the steps right behind.

It's going to be a long two days.

While Yutaka seemed fluent in English, his conversational skills left Richard wondering if the Japanese agent had ever talked with a native speaker in the language. After Richard settled into the bench in their compartment, he attempted to be more cordial with his assigned companion.

"Have you traveled much outside of Japan?" Richard asked.

Yutaka shook his head before opening a newspaper and reading it.

"I guess we're just going to do this as enemies instead of friends," Richard said. "I'd much rather have an escort who isn't afraid to speak to me."

"We'll get along fine if you stop talking," Yutaka said, punctuating his statement with a grunt.

Richard ignored Yutaka's jab. "I'm really interested in experiencing some of the local cuisines. What would you recommend? I've heard something about a dish called sushi."

Yutaka shot a glance at Richard over the top of the newspaper before returning to reading.

"What about any festivals? Are there any celebrations that will be taking place over the next week?"

Yutaka put his paper down and leaned forward. "If you don't want me to throw you and your mail out of that window, be quiet."

"Not here to be my friend," Richard said. "Got it."

The train lurched forward, catching Richard by surprise. He steadied himself and then stared out the window.

For the next couple hours, Richard took in the awe-inspiring Ryohaku mountain range and the rural Japanese countryside. He quickly forgot about his yearning to return home, instead appreciating the opportunity to visit Japan with each passing moment. Drinking in the shifting landscape, he wondered how so much beauty could be contained on such a small island. Then he wondered why Japan wasn't prioritized any higher on his list of places to visit.

Feeling parched, he announced that he was going to the dining car to get something to drink. Yutaka folded up his paper and fell in line behind Richard.

"I can bring you back something," Richard said. "It's not like there's anywhere for me to escape from you."

"Where you go, I go."

"Fair enough, but if you're going to always be with me, you're going to have to talk to me. I can't have this silence nonsense."

Yutaka said nothing.

"Are you married? Do you have any children?"

"No."

"Now we're getting somewhere," Richard said. "What city were you born in?"

"Nagasaki."

"And what brought you to the main island?"

"Work," Yutaka said. "There's more criminal activity here."

"Well, I can assure you that there's nothing criminal going on here," Richard said. "Trust me, I'm just a young man delivering some mail."

"I don't trust anyone."

Richard sighed. "Would you like a drink?"

"I'll buy my own."

Before attempting more torturous conversation with Yutaka, Richard looked across the car and gasped.

No, it can't be.

But before he could get another look at the woman he thought looked like Hisako, a commotion across the room arrested almost everyone's attention. Richard didn't understand the woman's rantings and instead craned his neck to see if he could get another look at Hisako. She seemed to disappear in the sea of people milling around the bar. He glanced at Yutaka, who was captivated by the woman waving her arms around as she related a story.

Seconds later, everyone was rushing in the direction she pointed.

Yutaka grabbed Richard's arm, pulling him toward the exit.

"What are you doing?" Richard asked. "I haven't even got my drink."

"It can wait," Yutaka said. "There's been a murder."

CHAPTER 6

Maibara, Japan

WHEN THE TRAIN CAME TO A STOP AT THE MAIBARA station, police flooded the cars in a matter of minutes. Richard watched from his cabin as the conductor paced back and forth outside, ensuring that all passengers remained on board for the duration of the investigation. Yutaka shut the door and ordered Richard to stay put in an effort to contain him before hustling off to assist the other officers. An hour passed before Richard got up and eased the window down. He stuck his head in the fresh air and drew in a deep breath.

The conductor scowled and shouted something in Japanese at Richard.

"What?" Richard asked.

"Stay inside," the man said.

"I just needed some fresh air."

Richard ignored the directions and watched snow fall fast, coating the exposed portion of the platform in a matter of minutes.

The conductor drew nearer to Richard. "Get inside now."

"Okay, okay," Richard said. "I'm not going anywhere. I've never been to Japan, so I'm trying to enjoy as much of it as I can."

"Inside now," the man repeated.

This time, Richard complied, easing back into his compartment and then raising the window. Once he finished, he heard someone rapping on the opaque glass. He spun around to see the outline of a dark figure.

"Can I help you?" Richard asked after sliding open the door.

"Officer Yutaka asked me to come speak with you," the man said. He wore a long trench coat and a bowler hat.

"Did he?" Richard asked, his eyes widening. "Up until a few minutes ago, the officer has been with me everywhere except when I used the restroom. He's a little obsessive if you know what I mean."

The man didn't even crack a smile.

"Where were you in the minutes before the body was discovered?" the man asked, twirling his pen as he did, awaiting a response he could record.

"I was with Yutaka in this cabin," Richard said. "Didn't he vouch for me already?"

"He only told me that he suspected you in some way."

"That's absurd," Richard said. "How on Earth could I get close enough to him to kill the victim anyway?"

"I never underestimate my enemies."

Richard cocked his head to one side and furrowed his brow. "You believe that I'm your enemy?"

The man nodded.

Richard chuckled. "Not even close. I don't know your name, inspector, but that's quite an assumption to make without considering the facts."

"Inspector Niko," the man said. "And I'm trying to figure out what happened here. The facts are that you have been deemed a suspicious person since you set foot in our country. So, what are you hiding, Mr.—"

"Halliburton. Richard Halliburton. And if you think I'm hiding something, you'd be mistaken. And as far as being a murder suspect, I've been tethered to Yutaka's hip for the past day. Or did he not tell you?"

"He mentioned it."

"Then how could I have done it without him noticing?"

The man scribbled down a note on his pad. "Officer Yutaka mentioned that you did go to the bathroom a half-hour before the murder victim was found."

"Yes, but the officer was in the bathroom with me. I couldn't have slipped past him without being noticed."

"Did you know the victim?"

Halliburton shrugged. "I don't even know if it's a man or a woman, though I am curious about how the victim died."

"Knife wound. Do you have such a weapon stashed in your belongings somewhere?"

Richard grabbed his bag and then tossed it at the inspector's feet. "Be my guest. Have a look."

The man knelt to unzip the luggage. He rifled through the contents before growling. After sliding the bag toward the corner, he rose and surveyed the room.

"See," Richard said. "I told you."

"What about those mail pouches?"

"I would allow you to look through those, but I'm afraid I can't do that. I don't want you rummaging through personal correspondence."

The man fell back to the ground and scooped up both bags.

"Sir, perhaps you didn't hear me," Richard said.

The inspector looked up at Richard and glared. "Are you going to stop me?"

"Please, sir. I'm begging you."

Ignoring his pleas, the inspector sifted through the

pouches. After a couple minutes, he cinched the sacks and tossed them aside before proceeding to search beneath the benches and rummaging through the closet.

Satisfied that the room was devoid of the murder weapon, the man exited without saying a word. A half-hour later, Yutaka returned to the compartment and settled into the seat across from Richard.

"Well," Richard said. "Did you catch who did it?"

Yutaka nodded. "The killer was caught."

The train's brakes hissed as steam filled the platform.

"Wow," Richard said before his mouth fell agape. "The speed at which Japanese law enforcement works is most impressive. Where I'm from, this train would've remained here for days along with all the passengers as everyone was thoroughly interrogated and the murder weapon was in hand."

"Japan is not like America."

"Not when it comes to solving crime. I mean, we have some incredible detectives, but that kind of speed was unprecedented. So, where did you find the murder weapon?"

"We didn't."

Richard leaned forward and carefully eyed Yutaka. "So you're convinced you caught the murderer without finding the man in possession of the weapon?"

"That's right."

"Maybe your standard for convicting a person is lower here."

"It's easy when the man confesses."

"He confessed?" Richard asked.

"Admitted to everything. Once we cornered him, he had no other choice but to tell the truth or bring further shame upon his family."

"And you're confident you have the right man?"

Yutaka remained silent as he stared out the window.

"All right, sir. I'll take your word for it. Just not how I would've done things."

"No one asked for your opinion."

Richard threw his hands in the air. "I know. I'm sorry. Didn't mean to offend your procedure here. Just not how I'm used to seeing things done. Kind of surprising, that's all."

The station disappeared as the train built up speed.

Fifteen minutes later, Richard stood and stretched. "So, about that drink we were going to get—"

"Let's go," Yutaka said as he gestured toward the door.

Richard slid it open and exited first with Yutaka close behind. When they reached the dining car, the two men sauntered up to the bar to order a drink.

"What do you recommend?" Richard asked Yutaka.

"You can't go wrong with nihonshu,"

"Nihonshu? What is that?"

"Rice wine," Yutaka said. "I believe you Americans call it sake."

Richard smiled and slapped the counter. "Well, that's what I want then."

When they received their drinks, Richard noticed Hisako standing on the other side of the room. He wanted to speak with her but wasn't sure how he could casually pass her a note without arousing suspicion from Yutaka.

Richard picked up a pen lying on the bar and began doodling on a napkin. After a few minutes, Yutaka turned his attention elsewhere, clearly bored with Richard's scrawling. Richard flipped over the napkin and wrote down "22:00" and "Room 17", his cabin number. He hoped she would figure out what everything meant.

An hour later, Richard and Yutaka were back in the cabin, the former engrossed in a book picked up while on

The Ardent, the latter skimming a newspaper.

At two minutes to 10:00 p.m., Richard walked over to the closet. He'd noticed a thin piece of exposed metal earlier on the door. He dragged his finger along the sharp edge, drawing blood.

"Oww," Richard before he grabbed his finger. "I cut myself."

Yutaka peered at Richard's hands. "Let me see."

Richard revealed the bloody mess. "Can you get me a bandage for this? It really hurts."

"Don't go anywhere," Yutaka said.

"We're on a moving train. You think I'm going to jump out?"

"Maybe."

"I'm not stupid."

Yutaka grunted before exiting the room.

One minute later, there was a knock on the door. Richard slid it open to find Hisako. He gestured for her to join him inside.

"Quickly," he said.

"What a surprise," she said.

Richard narrowed his eyes. "What did you do to me back on the ship?"

She glanced at his hand. "What happened?"

"Never mind that," he said. "I want to know what you did to me."

"What do you mean?"

"You know exactly what I mean. You gave me that tea and the next thing I know, I wake up and the ship was already in port."

"You were tired from too much dancing."

"I wasn't born that long ago, but it wasn't yesterday."

She shrugged. "I put something in your tea."

Richard glared at her. "And the cipher?"

"The what?"

"Don't play dumb. You put something in my tea so you could go into my room, didn't you?"

"That's what I was assigned to do."

"So, where is the cipher?"

"I gave it back to the man who told me to steal it from you."

"And who's that?"

"A very powerful man, someone you don't want to tangle with."

"Look, I don't have much time," Richard said. "There's someone watching me to make sure I deliver this mail to Tokyo. But he thinks I'm here for other reasons."

"And he's right, isn't he?"

Richard shook his head. "You can't be here when he gets back. So, we need to continue this conversation later."

"Why should I be worried about him? What's he going to do to me?"

"I'm already going to be in trouble because of what you stole from me on that ship and—"

Hisako smiled. "Taking something back that belongs to you isn't stealing."

"Just go, and we'll finish this in the dining car."

As she walked toward the door, Richard heard footsteps just outside.

"That man can't see you in here," Richard said. "He'll be more suspicious of me than ever."

"That's not my problem."

"Please, Hisako. Get in the closet."

She didn't move as the door slid open.

CHAPTER 7

RICHARD STEPPED IN FRONT OF HISAKO AS YUTAKA slid open the door. He eyed Richard closely, looking him up and down before attempting to see who was behind him.

"I know this looks suspicious," Richard said, placing his hands in the air in a gesture of surrender, "but I can explain."

Hisako put her head inside, her dark straight hair hiding her face.

"It looks like you found a friend," Yutaka said, turning his gaze toward Hisako. "Now, get out."

Richard shifted his weight from one foot to the other. "Look, she knocked on the door and—"

"I don't care," Yutaka said, still staring at Hisako. "You need to leave now."

Hisako slipped past the two men without looking up and then disappeared into the hall.

"What was that all about?" Yutaka asked.

"There was a knock at the door, and I thought it was you," Richard said. "So, I opened it. And before I could say anything, she pushed her way inside."

"Be careful who you let inside on this train," Yutaka said.

"What's that supposed to mean? I thought you caught the killer."

"People are never who they seem to be."

"Does that apply to you too?" Richard asked.

"Just keep the door shut next time. Now let me see your cut."

Richard held out his hand, which Yutaka promptly bandaged.

"Don't be so careless next time," he said.

* * *

THE TRAIN CHUGGED into the Nagoya station for an extended stop. Richard wanted to get out and explore for a few minutes, if anything to chat with some of the people on the platform hawking their wares to a captivated audience of entrapped passengers. He lifted the window and signaled for a boy to come over only to have Yutaka spring up and slam it down.

"It's rude to call him over if you don't intend to buy anything," he said.

"I just wanted to talk."

"That's right—and you'd be stealing his time away from someone who might sincerely want to purchase what he's selling."

"What is that he's chanting anyway? 'Yaki imo'?"

Yutaka nodded. "It's a sweet potato, cooked over a wood fire."

"Well, now I want one. That reminds me of home."

"You eat sweet potatoes in America?"

"My mother makes the best ones you'll ever put in your mouth, especially when the butter is just starting to melt."

The corners of Yutaka's lips turned slightly upward for the first time since he'd joined Richard. "Then go ahead. Call him over again. I shouldn't deprive anyone the great Japanese delicatessen of yaki imo."

Richard lifted the window and whistled at the boy.

When he came over, Richard bought a yaki imo from the kid and added a little extra for tip. Seconds later, Richard burned the roof of his mouth on the sweet potato.

"Slow down, my friend," Yutaka said, breaking into a chuckle. "They're very hot."

Richard blew on his food and then watched the steam drift upward. "You need to warn me earlier next time."

"Perhaps you should simply exercise more patience in your life."

Richard shook his head. "If I had a nickel for every time someone told me that, I would be riding in first class right now."

"Maybe you should start listening to them."

After a half-hour, Richard started to wonder why the train hadn't moved. He got up and stuck his head outside, looking in both directions.

"How long is this stop supposed to last?" he asked.

Yutaka shrugged. "Normally twenty minutes to a half-hour."

"We've been sitting here longer than that."

Yutaka wandered over to the window and gestured for the conductor to come closer. The man strode over to meet them. For the next couple minutes, the two men had a conversation in Japanese, leaving Richard with nothing to do but watch them banter back and forth. Finally, the conductor left.

"What is it?" Richard asked.

"Grab your bags," Yutaka said. "We need to go."

"Go where? What's happening?"

"The train has some mechanical issues that need to be fixed elsewhere. They will bring a new train in tomorrow evening, and we can board it then."

"So, what are we supposed to do between now and then?"

"They're going to make an announcement that the train company is putting us up for the night in the Izumi Mori hotel."

"I won't complain about sleeping on a bed tonight."

"Who says you're going to sleep on the bed?" Yutaka said. "I'm not letting you out of my sight. We will share a room together. And you will sleep on the floor."

Richard sighed. "Just when I was starting to like you, Yutaka."

What started out as a grunt from Yutaka, turned into a laugh. "You'll survive."

Richard snatched up the mail pouches off the floor along with his bag and followed Yutaka to the hotel. As they continued along the street, Richard heard an announcement broadcast by the conductor followed by loud groans.

"Doesn't sound like they're happy about the news that we're staying in Nagoya tonight," Richard said.

"Are you happy?" Yutaka asked.

"No, but only because I can't get out and see this incredible country. I feel like a prisoner traveling with you."

"It's really that bad?"

"Look, I want to explore Japan. Being cooped up in a car like cattle isn't how I wanted to see your land."

Yutaka nodded. "I'll make a deal with you. You leave your mail with me in the morning, and I'll let you go."

"How do I know you won't read it?"

"You don't, but there has to be some level of trust on both our parts for this to work. You have to trust I won't read every letter. And I have to trust that you'll come back."

"Sounds fair enough."

"Good," Yutaka said. "Leave the mail with me tomorrow, and go enjoy Nagoya."

Richard smiled at the proposal, but he wasn't about to leave the mail alone with Yutaka, not even for a minute.

* * *

THE NEXT MORNING, Richard awoke, keen on escaping the watchful eye of Yutaka. However, the proposal he made the night before wasn't enticing. But instead of complaining, Richard gave off the impression that he would entertain Yutaka's idea.

While Yutaka was in the bathroom, Richard swapped out the mail from the sacks with literature he collected in the lobby the previous evening. He stuffed the mail into a laundry bag and then hustled out of the room.

In the lobby, Richard asked a porter to keep his luggage and laundry sack safe and away from the prying eyes of Yutaka, tipping the man far more than usual. Richard didn't waste any time before heading to an onsen to soak.

When he arrived at the bathhouse, he got undressed and eased into the warm water. Several men were relaxing against the edge, engaged in conversation. Richard found a spot to himself and reveled in the moment. He needed the break after all the rough travel he'd endured over the past few days. And sleeping on the floor at the foot of Yutaka's bed didn't help matters either.

After a few minutes, one of the men looked at Richard and spoke to him in English.

"What brings you to Nagoya?" the man asked.

Richard glanced around the pool and then pointed at himself. "Are you asking me?"

The man nodded.

"I hadn't planned on stopping here. And to be honest, I'd never even heard of Nagoya until last night when our train broke down here on the way to Tokyo. But I'm making the most of it."

The two continued in cordial banter for a few minutes before Richard heard a familiar voice coming from down the hallway.

Yutaka!

Richard climbed out of the water and hustled back to the changing room. He went to grab a towel, but couldn't find one. His clothes were lying scattered around a bench. As he attempted to put his pants back on, he heard Yutaka's voice getting nearer.

Without enough time to grab all his clothes, Richard dove into one of the stalls and waited. He peered through a crack in the doors.

Yutaka spoke in Japanese to a bath house employee before scooping up Richard's clothes. The man said something to Yutaka, and then they both marched out into the hallway.

Richard took a deep breath and exited the stall. He grabbed a towel and wrapped it around his waist before peering out into the hallway. To the right, Yutaka was engaged in a conversation with the employee. Behind them were a couple of police officers scanning the area. And to the left was the women's pool.

It's not like I really have a choice.

Richard darted down the hallway and ducked into the women's changing room, which happened to be empty. Then he heard Yutaka's voice echoing off the walls.

Richard gritted his teeth before dashing into the women's pool. Several of the ladies shrieked and covered themselves with their hands. He put his index finger to his lips and winked at them.

"Richard!" Yutaka shouted as he stormed around the corner and burst into the room.

But Richard was nowhere to be found.

CHAPTER 8

RICHARD'S LUNGS BURNED AS HE HELD HIS BREATH. His dive beneath the warm water was made in faith, hoping that his charm would inspire the women to shield him from Yutaka. Through the water, he could hear Yutaka's deep voice growing louder as he undoubtedly demanded answers from the women. But between their shrieks and the language barrier, Richard had no idea what was happening. After about a minute, he felt a tap on his back.

Richard rose to the surface, gasping for air. The women were all lined against the side of the pool, pointing and smiling at him.

"Is he gone?" Richard asked.

One of the women responded in Japanese, but he didn't understand anything she said. He covered himself as he climbed out of the water and snatched his towel. Upon re-entering the changing room, Richard found a kimono along with a fur-lined winter coat. He didn't like stealing someone's belongings, but since Yutaka had scooped up Richard clothes, he did what he had to do.

Richard kept his feet close together, taking small steps as he shuffled past the onsen employees with his head down. Across the room, Richard saw an animated Yutaka, who was waving his arms as his voice escalated.

Once Richard left the public baths, he maintained his cover, scooting slowly along the edge of the street with the flow of foot traffic. He resisted the urge to buy another yaki imo as he passed several street vendors luring customers with the aroma of cooked sweet potatoes in the stiff evening breeze. While Richard wanted something to eat, he would've settled for a hot drink, anything to keep him warm amid the freezing temperatures.

He meandered back toward the hotel, taking a long route just so he could absorb more of the Japanese culture. However, as he turned the corner, he locked eyes with Hisako. Diverting his gaze elsewhere, he darted down a side street. However, when he glanced over his shoulder, Hisako was only a few feet behind him.

"That's a beautiful kimono," she said.

"This isn't how I left my hotel room this morning," he said.

"What happened?"

"You're only going to laugh at me. Why should I tell you?"

"Perhaps you're wrong," she said. "But you'll never know if you don't tell me."

"I went to an onsen this morning, and Yutaka tracked me there. I don't know how, but he managed to follow me to the baths."

Her eyebrows shot upward. "But you escaped?"

Richard nodded. "I did, wearing these clothes. Otherwise, he would've apprehended me."

"But you don't want to be caught, do you?"

"Of course not, at least not based on all the things you told me before. I need a new start, one that doesn't include some Japanese detective peering over my shoulder every second of my time here."

"So, this is your attempt to ditch him?"

Richard nodded.

"And how's that working for you so far?" she asked.

"There's room for improvement."

Before their conversation went any further, Hisako nudged Richard toward the nearby alley. "We need to get out of sight right now."

"Why? What's happening?"

"The police are coming."

"If I just keep my head down, I should—"

"Nothing is for certain, not today, not tomorrow. It's going to require more than a kimono to get away from Yutaka."

"And you're willing to help me?"

"Maybe," Hisako said. "For now, just don't act suspicious. Your opportunity to escape him will arrive soon enough. And when it does, you'll be ready for it."

"You sound quite confident," Richard said.

"That's the only way to be," she said.

"Right now I need to be anonymous."

The voice of men calling drew nearer.

"Is that the police again?" he asked.

Then Hisako kissed Richard, catching him by surprise as she pinned him to the wall. After a few seconds, the footfalls grew fainter and she pulled back.

Richard's eyes widened. "I wasn't expecting that."

"Did you like it?" she asked with a wink.

"You may have saved my life."

"There's something I need to tell you."

Richard furrowed his brow. "What is it?"

"The police aren't after you," she said. "They're after me."

CHAPTER 9

QUESTIONS FLOODED RICHARD'S MIND WITH HISAKO'S revelation. He wanted to know what she did to become the focus of a manhunt. He wanted to know how she intended to escape. He wanted to know everything. But there was no time.

Hisako yanked Richard's arm, pulling him deeper into the alley with her. He struggled to keep pace, his strides reduced by the limitations from the kimono. After stumbling a couple times, he stopped and ripped the bottom of the dress to create more flexibility.

"Better?" Hisako asked after Richard finished.

"Much better," he said while testing out his range of motion.

"Good. Let's keep moving."

They wound through a series of alleys before emerging onto the main street near their hotel. As they neared the entrance, she rerouted them to a cafe less than a hundred meters away. She ordered them two cups of tea and directed him to sit in the back corner of the eatery.

"What's going on?" Richard asked in a hushed tone.

She glanced around at the rest of the customers, who appeared to be engaged in conversation. "You're not being watched as closely as you think."

Richard furrowed his brow. "There's a man who's been

following me around ever since I set foot in this country. Seems kind of close to me."

"Japan has a spy in the American consulate in Japan," she said. "Their understanding is that your job was to deliver the cipher and that you're not actually here on any other mission."

"That's true."

"Yutaka will search for you, but once you get away from him, he's going to return to Tokyo for his next assignment. They know you'll be going straight to the embassy, and if they have reason to begin following you again, they will do it there."

"And you're sure about this?"

"I've been doing this long enough to know how Japanese intelligence works," she said.

A woman delivered a small tea pot and two mugs to their table along with tea leaves. Richard waited until she left before resuming conversation.

"Why are the authorities after you?" he asked.

"I was tasked with stealing the cipher from you and giving it to my contact. However, I heard that he now wants me dead."

"Dead? What did you do?"

"It's a long story."

Richard stirred his tea and rescued the tea leaves from the cup. "I've got plenty of time."

"Actually, you don't—and neither do I."

"Our train isn't supposed to leave until later tonight."

She pulled an envelope out of her purse. "That's why I bought us two tickets for the noon train to Tokyo."

"So, we've got about an hour to get back to the train station?"

She nodded. "That's why we need to get moving."

As she stood to leave, Richard grabbed her wrist. "Be honest. Why are you helping me?"

"My reasons aren't completely selfless. Honestly, my chances of escaping with you are greater than without. They're going to be searching for a woman by herself, but if we're together, we won't draw as much suspicion."

"Are you sure? We're both fugitives."

"Nobody but Yutaka is trying to track you down, but all the police in the city of Nagoya are on the lookout for me. If I'm with you, I won't be alone."

Richard stroked his chin as he considered his next move.

"We need to get going," she said as she stood.

He didn't budge. "If this is truly the case, why should I help you? After all, you were the one who stole the cipher from me."

"I was just doing my job, just like you were doing yours."

"Yes, but if I help you, what's in it for me? According to you, I have nothing to worry about once I get back on that train. From the way you're talking, Yutaka might as well be my best friend."

"I can prove to be valuable to you and your country. There's obviously some reason for concern if you're going through such much trouble to deploy agents to steal and smuggle a cipher into the consulate in Tokyo."

"I'm simply the messenger," Richard said. "I have no interest in the politics of espionage. To be completely frank, I only agreed to do this so I could force my handler to make good on his promise to help connect me with a publisher."

"You want to be a writer?"

"More than anything in the world."

"And are you writing about Japan?"

Richard nodded. "That's the plan."

"Then forget how much the consulate could use my help. If you're going to experience the fullness of all Japan has to offer, you need someone like me, someone who knows the geography and culture, not to mention someone who can speak fluent English."

"I'd prefer not to be in fear for my life the entire time I'm here."

"I'll become someone else," she said. "It won't be that difficult to do in Tokyo. They'll never find me again."

Richard took a deep breath then slowly exhaled as he mulled over her offer. Agreeing to Hisako's plan had plenty of advantages. If anything, she could help him get the most of his brief time in Japan, giving him the ability to parlay his experiences into multiple articles. The downside was also fraught with danger. If she was captured by the authorities and he was with her, it could spell doom for him as well. He weighed both sides for a moment before announcing his decision.

"You make a compelling case," Richard said. "And I've never been one to err on the side of caution."

"So you'll help me?" she asked.

Richard nodded. "Whatever you need until we get to Tokyo—then I need you to help me."

"Sounds like we have ourselves a deal. Now, let's go."

They scurried out of the cafe and kept their heads down, Richard keeping his covered. Fifteen minutes later, they approached the train station before he realized he couldn't leave the mail behind.

"I have to go back," he announced.

"Go back where? There's hardly any time."

"To the hotel. I need to get my bag and the mail pouches."

"We may not have enough time."

"I can't leave behind my bag. It's got all my notes."

Hisako growled. "Then let's speed it up."

Richard spun around and shuffled toward the hotel. Hisako hustled alongside him as they approached the front door.

"We need to stick together," she said.

"And I need to get out of this ridiculous dress."

However, as they entered the lobby, Richard looked up and saw Yutaka standing casually near the front desk, talking to one of the employees. Yutaka leaned close before handing the man some money.

Richard grabbed Hisako and turned her in the opposite direction.

"What are you doing?" she whispered.

"We've got a big problem."

CHAPTER 10

RICHARD USHERED HISAKO DOWN A HALLWAY NEAR THE lobby. He checked a couple of the doors leading into the dining area before finding one that opened. Nodding toward the room, she entered and he followed closely behind.

"What is it?" she asked. "I thought this was going to be simple. You grab your bags and we run back to the station."

"It was supposed to be," Richard said. "But Yutaka was handing money to the same guy I tipped to keep quiet about me."

"We have a proverb for that here: If he'll take money from you, he'll take money from everyone else."

"That's an actual proverb?"

She snickered. "No, but like all proverbs, it's common sense."

"Well, I didn't count on Yutaka to come snooping around. I just gave the man an extra big tip so he wouldn't announce what I did to everyone."

"Nothing we can do about that now," she said as she paced around him. "However, you're still wearing your kimono."

"You think I can just walk right up to that man and give him my claim ticket and he'll fetch my bags without turning me in?"

"What other option do you have?"

Richard shrugged. "And if he catches me, I'll be fine, at least according to you."

"But I won't be. So, do your best to make sure Yutaka doesn't see or hear you."

"Wish me luck."

She shoved some money into his hand. "Just in case."

Richard exited the room, shuffling along the hall toward the hotel's front desk. He kept his head covered and down as he neared the counter. Yutaka had moved a few feet away but was still scanning the lobby, his hands buried in his pants pockets.

He didn't look up when Richard arrived in front of the clerk. Richard slid the claims ticket in front of the hotel employee. When he returned a few seconds later, he wore a scowl on his face.

He said something in Japanese that Richard didn't understand. Instead of allowing the charade to continue, Richard locked eyes with the man and spoke softly and slowly in English.

"Did you lose my bags?"

"I'm sorry," the employee said, his eyes widening as he recognized Richard wasn't a woman. "I thought you were someone else and—"

"I am someone else," Richard replied. "I'm the guy who gave you those bags in the first place. There should be a total of three of them. And I need them all right now."

The man leaned forward on the counter, continuing in a hushed tone. "Someone just came here looking for you."

"I know," Richard said. "That's why I paid you to keep quiet about it. But you didn't, did you?"

The man shrugged. "He paid better. So, unless you're willing to give me more—"

Richard handed over all the money Hisako had given him. "That should be enough."

"Maybe," he said.

"That's all I have."

"He gave me twice that amount."

"I wish I had more to give you, but I don't have any more. I'm relying on good will the rest of my time in Japan, and it starts with you."

Moments later, the man spun and walked behind him. He put his shoulder into a closet door, forcing it open. When he re-emerged, had three bags. After placing them on the counter, he slapped the bell and looked at Richard.

"Here they are," the man said.

Richard snatched them off the counter and strode toward the exit. However, he didn't get far before he sensed someone standing in front of him. Richard didn't need to look up to know who it was.

Yutaka worked over a toothpick in his mouth as he circled around Richard.

"I'm not sure that dress suits you," Yutaka said.

Richard eyed Yutaka closely before juking around him.

"Teishi! Teishi!" Yutaka shouted.

Richard caught a glimpse of Hisako out of the corner of his eye as he darted outside. While he didn't waste precious time looking back to see where Yutaka was, Richard could hear the thundering footsteps drawing nearer. Richard was convinced he could outrun Yutaka under normal circumstances. But hindered by the tight kimono, Richard struggled to put much distance between him and his pursuer.

Up ahead, he noticed a corner and dashed around it before spinning around, cocking his arms behind his head. He listened for any indication that Yutaka was about to catch up. But Yutaka never arrived.

Richard peered around the corner to see what might have happened when he noticed Hisako straddling Yutaka, who was laid out on his back on the pavement. She had her heel on his throat.

"No," Richard shouted.

Hisako paused and looked up. "I could take care of him right now."

"Let him go," Richard said. "We're running out of time."

Richard dashed back into the alley and furiously dug through his bag. He located an outfit before stripping down and then changing.

"Ready?" she asked as he looked down the sidewalk to see Yutaka staggering to his feet.

"What'd you do?" Richard asked as they broke into a sprint.

"Gave him a taste of his own medicine," she said.

They didn't break stride until they arrived on the platform. Hisako presented the two tickets to the conductor and hustled on board.

"I need to get into a different dress," she said. "The less we look like we did ten minutes ago, the better. In fact, I suggest you change, too."

Richard growled but complied, donning his third shirt in the past half hour.

"Not your style?" she asked with a chuckle.

"I prefer something not so stuffy," he said as he straightened the tie he'd just whipped around his collar. "Is there anything wrong with that?"

"You'd make a terrible Japanese man."

"Hopefully I'd make a better Japanese man than I did a Japanese woman."

She shrugged. "You were just starting to perfect that

shuffle while wearing your kimono."

Richard finished dressing and then discussed strategy with Hisako for if the police made the rounds.

A few minutes later, there was loud rapping on their cabin door.

"Ready?" she asked him.

"Wish me luck," he said.

"Good luck," she mouthed before turning toward the door.

"Please open up," the conductor said.

* * *

HISAKO TUGGED HER BLOUSE taut before easing up to the door. "Who is it?" she asked in Japanese.

"The conductor."

She slid open the panel, revealing Yutaka standing next to the conductor.

"He's not here," Hisako said. "And I'm not sure if I'll ever see him again."

"Did you kill him?"

She shook her head. "Nothing like that. He's just quite the free spirit. He only came here to see Japan, not to cause any trouble. I'm afraid he got caught up in something that he didn't anticipate."

"That doesn't excuse his actions," Yutaka said. "My assignment was to watch him, but now he's broken several laws and things have changed. I need to see inside your cabin."

"All aboard," an assistant conductor outside bellowed.

The train jerked as it started to move.

"I already told you that he's not here," Hisako said. "But if you must, see for yourself."

Yutaka pushed his way past Hisako, barely able to squeeze his portly frame past her in the tight quarters. He searched all over cabin, inspecting the closets and beneath the bed before cursing.

"I know he was here," Yutaka said.

"Sometimes, we see what we want to see."

Yutaka sighed and then narrowed his eyes as his gaze met Hisako. "I'm only going to give you one more chance to tell me where he is."

"Or then what?"

"I know the authorities are looking for you."

"Yet I'm not the one you're looking for. What a shame for you."

Yutaka clenched both his fists and pursed his lips. "You tell me where he is right now or I'm going to take you in myself."

The train hissed before it started to chug forward.

"I don't believe you have a ticket and we're leaving the station," she said.

"Makes no difference to me. Now, you tell me where Richard Halliburton is or I'm going to make your life quite miserable."

Hisako sat down on the bed and patted the space next to her. "Please, have a seat."

"Do you require my assistance anymore?" the conductor asked. "If not, I have other business to attend to."

Yutaka nodded. "I can handle this."

Once the conductor left, Yutaka slid the door shut and feigned as if he was going to sit down next to Hisako. But then he turned to face her before slamming his hand over her mouth and forcing her onto her back. Hisako squealed as she fought Yutaka. After a brief struggle, she squirmed free and scrambled to her feet on the other side of the cabin.

"Where is he?" Yutaka said.

"I wouldn't advise touching me again like that."

"Have it your way," he said before pulling out his knife. "You're coming with me."

"You think Im going to jump off a moving train with you?"

"No, but you're going to sit with me until we arrive in Tokyo."

He reached for her arm, but she pulled it away. "This isn't a game."

She sighed and then spoke through a clenched jaw. "Fine. I'll tell you where he is."

"Thank you," Yutaka said, still wielding his knife.

"Put the weapon away, please," she said. "He's not going to hurt you."

"It's not him I'm worried about," Yutaka said.

Outside the streetlamps around Nagoya flickered as the train gained speed. She knew there wasn't much time.

"He's outside," she said.

"Outside?"

"Yes," she said. "He climbed through the window. Let me show you."

Hisako walked over to the window to slide it upward. She poked her head out and gave Richard a knowing look.

"Let me see," Yutaka said, pulling her aside so he could see Richard for himself.

"Well, hello, Mr. Halliburton," Yutaka said. "It's time you come back inside here and we have a little chat."

"If you insist," Richard said. "I just need a hand."

Yutaka offered his hand, but instead of allowing him to provide any help, Richard yanked hard, pulling Yutaka thought he opening. Just as they had discussed in their plan, Hisako sprang into action. She shoved Yutaka in his rear end, ramming him through the tight opening in the window.

In a flash, she and Richard were workmanlike with their

push-and-pull strategy. They needed less than a minute to get Yutaka more than halfway out of the portal. After that, they only needed to nudge him, sending him plunging headlong into the shrubbery along the tracks.

They barely had any time to celebrate their victory when Hisako cringed and shouted.

"Richard! Look out!"

He turned around to see a tunnel fast approaching.

CHAPTER 11

RICHARD'S HANDS DRIPPED WITH SWEAT AS HE SWUNG into action. After clinging to the railing on the top of the passenger car while the train started moving, his arms were on fire. Adrenaline coursed through his body as he eyed the oncoming tunnel.

"Get in here now," Hisako said.

"I'm trying," Richard said while repositioning himself.

He figured he only had time for one try and needed to ensure that he generated enough momentum to swing inside.

"Come on, Richard," Hisako said.

He gritted his teeth and prepared to make his move.

One . . . two . . . three . . .

When Richard swung his legs down into the window, he overshot his target. His feet hit the side of the train with a thud, prompting more outcries from Hisako.

"Richard!"

With the train running out of track before the tunnel, he didn't have a chance to consider the consequences, acting solely on instinct. He drew his legs back up and flung them downward. This time, they flew into the opening. He slithered inside, aided by Hisako, who pulled on his feet as soon as they entered the cabin.

Richard hit the floor hard as darkness enveloped the room. Lying flat on his back, he exhaled and muttered a short prayer, thankful that he survived such an ordeal.

"You almost got yourself killed out there," Hisako said.

"I didn't have much of a choice, did I?"

"Let's just focus on the fact that you're alive and Yutaka is gone."

Richard sat up as his eyes started to adjust. Then a flicker of light blinded him for a moment as Hisako lit a cigarette.

"Do you want one?" she asked.

"Not right now," he said. "I'm still trying to catch my breath."

"Did you see Yutaka hit the ground?"

"Yeah, it looked like a rough landing, but he was still moving."

"Good."

Richard furrowed his brow. "Good? Won't he try to find me in Tokyo?"

"That's still a possibility, but you would have more problems if he'd died. The agent assigned to watch you ended up dead with no witnesses. Just who do you think they would blame for such an act?"

"I suppose we'll find out soon enough," Richard said. "But in the meantime, I want to get this mail to the embassy before everyone tries to arrest me."

"We'll be there soon enough," she said.

"But not so soon that you can't tell me why someone wants you dead," he said.

The train exited the tunnel, and the cabin brightened from the noonday sun hanging high over the clear skies.

She blew a large plume of smoke upward and stared out the window. Quiet for a moment, she started to pace around before responding.

"I'm not a good person," she finally said. "A good spy?

Perhaps. But a good person? I'm no such thing."

"What do you mean?" he asked.

"I do awful things, terrible things. And I hate myself for doing it."

"Being a spy is simply a job. I mean, sure, there are times when duty requires you to do some unseemly things, but that doesn't make you an awful person."

"It's what I did to become a spy."

"And what was that?" Richard asked.

"I still can't talk about it. But just know that I'm not a good person because of it."

"If you don't want to talk about it, I'm not going to pressure you to," he said. "But I still would like to know why someone wants you dead. Did you complete your mission?"

She nodded. "I love my country, but not enough to do what I do for it. The risk of putting my life in danger to gather information for Japan's military isn't worth the reward."

"So, why work so hard to become a spy?"

She held the cigarette between her fingers before drawing it to her lips. Her cheeks sank as she sucked in a long drag.

"Revenge," she said coldly.

"Revenge? What happened to you?"

"It wasn't what happened to me. It was my mother."

"Your mother?"

Hisako nodded. "She was murdered by one of Prince Naruhiko's men a few years ago. I vowed to avenge her death, no matter what it cost me. I lost my childhood, living on the streets as an orphan because some spy didn't like the way my mother looked at him. He stabbed her right there on the sidewalk. And nobody said a thing to him."

"You watched it happen?"

She nodded. "Imagine watching your entire world collapse in front of your eyes while you're helpless to do anything about it. That's what it was like for me as she crumpled to the ground. Eventually she succumbed to the wounds, but she never had a chance."

"And did you complete your mission?"

"That's why they're after me," she said. "I'm assuming they finally found the murder weapon. Apparently, they want to interrogate me, but I've been in this business long enough to know what's really going to happen. Once they ask me a few questions, they're going to determine I'm guilty and then immediately execute me."

"But that's just conjecture. You don't know exactly what they have."

"Like I said, I'm good at reading between the lines. Prince Naruhiko is ruthless. He wouldn't hesitate to slash my throat, given the opportunity and the justification to do so."

Richard watched a tear trickle down her cheek. "What do you plan to do when you get to Tokyo?"

"Hide as best I can until they've forgotten about me."

"When will that be?" he asked.

"When I'm dead, if I'm lucky. I wouldn't be surprised if those monsters dug my body up just to try and kill me again."

"We can't let that happen."

She chuckled. "You and what army is going to stop them? You have no idea how powerful these people are."

"I didn't say I plan on stopping them personally, but as my grandma likes to say, 'There's more than one way to skin a cat.'"

"What is that supposed to mean?"

"Whenever there's a problem, there are multiple solutions."

She shrugged. "Maybe, but talking to Prince Naruhiko isn't one of them. And if he captures me, I doubt I'll live to see the next sunrise."

"Not with an attitude like that, but I'm betting that what you know will be valuable enough to the American government that they will protect you."

"I'm not sure if—"

"Stop selling yourself short. You are an incredible spy. I mean, you stole the cipher from me."

She gasped as she stood, holding her index finger in the air. "I've got a way to guarantee that your government will want to help me."

"And how do you intend to do that?"

"I'm going to help you get the cipher back."

* * *

LATER THAT NIGHT, the train pulled into the station in Tokyo. Richard made plans to rendezvous with Hisako the following afternoon to discuss her plan on how to retrieve the cipher. He remained somewhat cautious with her, unsure of where her true loyalty rested. After spending as much time as he had with her already, he realized her deepest devotion was to herself. And while he figured he could still work with her, he determined to do so with a good measure of trepidation.

Richard went to the hotel the embassy in Vladivostok had recommended.

"We've been expecting you, Mr. Halliburton," the man at the front desk said.

Richard smiled. "That's nice. Is the room already paid for?"

"Yes, but I'm afraid you won't be spending the night in it."

"What do you mean? I thought—" Richard stopped when he saw the man cut his eyes to his left and right.

"Mr. Halliburton," a man beside Richard said, "my name is Inspector Sato, and we'd like to have a word with you."

"Give me a moment. I need to put my things away."

Three men surrounded Richard, all dressed in suits. The one addressing Richard put his hands on his hips, pushing back his jacket.

"We can take those things for you," Sato said.

"I'm sorry," Richard said, "but it's been a really long day. I'd like to at least spend a couple minutes getting refreshed in my room before you take me anywhere."

"If you insist, but my men will be outside the door and in the street below."

"You have nothing to worry about," Richard said. "I have nowhere to go."

Richard lugged his bags upstairs to the third floor. As soon as he shut the door, he sprang into action. While he'd lost the cipher, the most important part of his mission, Richard didn't want to be a double disappointment to the U.S. embassy by also losing the mail.

Richard pulled his pocketknife out of bag and cut a slit in the mattress just wide enough to accept a letter. He proceeded to feed them inside one by one until both bags were emptied.

"What's taking so long, Mr. Halliburton?" Sato asked. "We need to question you quickly."

"I understand," Richard said. "However, you can't rush Mother Nature."

"I'm afraid I don't understand."

Richard chuckled. "I'll explain in a moment."

He buzzed around the room, putting everything back in place before finally opening the door.

"Ready?" Sato asked.

Richard nodded. "So, what is the reason for this inquiry? Is this typical for when Americans visit Tokyo?"

"We randomly inspect visitors on occasion to ensure that no contraband is being smuggled into the country. And we received a report that you might be carrying mail that wasn't properly checked upon arrival."

"I don't have any mail," Richard said.

Sato cocked his head to one side. "Did I receive a false report?"

"Apparently so, sir," Richard said.

As Sato commanded the other two men in Japanese, he glared at Richard. They rushed around the room, looking in every nook and cranny as Richard casually watched with a wry grin on his face.

"Do you find something about this amusing, Mr. Halliburton?" Sato asked.

Richard shrugged. "I could save you plenty of time if you would just listen to me. Didn't I already tell you that you're not going to find anything in this room?"

Sato strode up to Richard, getting within a few inches of his face. Richard didn't flinch.

"I don't trust Americans," Sato said.

"That's strange because as a general rule, Americans are kind-hearted and trusting people who'd give the shirt off their back for someone in need. At least that's been my experience, but maybe you've spent more time there than I have."

Sato moved uncomfortably closer. "Is this a joke to you?"

"There's one thing in life I don't find funny," Richard said. "And that's wasting time. Who knows just how much time we have to spend on this Earth? Personally, I don't want to squander even a second. So, while I might be smiling, I'm more miffed that you think it's necessary to tear apart my room, a room I just checked into ten minutes ago, in search of something that you're just not going to find. These are precious seconds I won't be able to get back, gone forever."

For the next couple minutes, Sato didn't budge, standing nose to nose with Richard. The move would have been intimidating to most, but Richard found it an obnoxious show of bravado. However, he knew characterizing Sato in his book would be a challenge. Readers might find the Japanese inspector over the top, prompting Richard to consider toning down Sato's brash personality when the time came to write about him.

One of the other men said something in Japanese to Sato, who huffed as he backed away from Richard.

"We will be watching you," Sato said. "If you make one slip, I will be there to catch you."

Richard shrugged. "I'm only here to share your incredibly beautiful country with the world in a new book. If you can help me with that, I will be most grateful."

"I will help keep you out of prison as long as you don't—how do you Americans say it?—stick your nose where it doesn't belong?"

"That's one of my favorite sayings," Richard said. "I find that to be a wonderful one to apply to your life. I've found that minding my own business keeps me focused on my own happiness instead of worrying about what others think. It's quite freeing and sound advice for everyone."

"I know you have contraband," Sato said. "I will catch you, too. And when I do, you'll find that it's difficult to write in a Japanese prison."

"Thank you for the visit, Inspector," Richard said before gesturing toward the door. "I'm assuming there won't be any need for further questioning."

"Not at this time, but that might change."

"Have a good evening, gentlemen," Richard said before he shut the door.

He put his back to the wall and slid to the floor, exhaling in relief. Richard hadn't been in Tokyo for more than a couple of hours and he was being placed under surveillance. He got up and meandered onto his balcony before his mouth fell agape.

On the clear and chilly January night, the moon hung low and bright on the horizon while the light created a crisp silhouette of Mt. Fuji.

That's why I'm here. Not to deliver ciphers. Not to relay diplomatic messages. I'm here to climb Mt. Fuji.

For the next fifteen minutes, Richard didn't move, soaking in all the grandeur available by moonlight. He finally decided to go to bed, anxious to see the snow-capped peaks at daybreak.

* * *

AFTER TAKING IN the majestic view of Mt. Fuji at dawn, Richard placed a few clothes in a sack designated for dirty clothes. Meanwhile, he retrieved all the letters and stuffed them into his bag, which he flung over his left shoulder.

When he exited the room, one of Sato's men was sitting in a chair in the hallway. He said something in Japanese that Richard didn't understand. Richard offered the man the laundry sack. After he unzipped it and inspected the contents, the man waved Richard down the hall.

"Have a wonderful day," Richard said, waving the laundry in one hand to distract him from the other bag. The ruse worked.

Once Richard reached the stairs, he dropped off his clothes with the front desk and continued to the embassy. As he walked down the sidewalk, he noticed a pair of men following him. Richard wasted little time in losing them, doubling back before reaching the embassy gates without incident.

Richard's greeting party consisted of the ambassador, Harold Newton, and the director of the consulate, Peter Ford. A smoldering cigar hung out of Newton's mouth, while Ford held a mug of steaming coffee.

"Just the man we've been waiting for," Newton said, slapping Richard on the back as he walked up the steps to the entrance.

"Thank you, sir," Richard said. "It's an honor to be here."

"Come on inside," Ford said, ushering him into Newton's office. "Let me know if there's anything I can get you. How were your accommodations last night?"

"Excellent," Richard said. "I haven't slept that well in a week, though I have been staying in cramped quarters on a boat and in a train car."

"That always makes your visit better," Ford said.

"Well, welcome to paradise," Newton said. "And from what I hear, you're about to crack open the lid on how incredible this place is, ruining it for everyone else."

"I wouldn't exactly put it like that, but I do intend to write about what a wonderful country this is."

"Have a seat," Newton said, gesturing toward a chair across from his desk. "Let's talk."

"Yes," Ford said. "Let's get down to business first. Let's see the cipher."

Richard sighed. "About that. I'm afraid I have some bad news."

Newton pulled the cigar out of his mouth and narrowed his eyes. "You better not have lost that thing. You know one of our best men died trying to deliver that to us?"

Richard closed his eyes and shook his head. "I'm sorry, sir. The Japanese had a spy on the ship. She put something in my tea, took my room key, and stole the device."

"And the letters?" Ford asked.

"I've got them right here," Richard said.

Newton cursed as he paced around the room. "We needed that cipher. Foster said you were the best man for the job. We paid for you to do one thing, and you failed."

"I understand that, sir, but there is a way to get it back," Richard said.

"And how do you expect to do that?" Newton said as he scowled. "I doubt you even know your way around the city yet."

"I'm going to have some help, but only on one condition."

"And what's that?"

"When I retrieve the cipher, you help the woman gain a new identity."

Newton furrowed his brow. "Who exactly is this woman? A spy?"

Richard paused, unsure of how he was going to navigate his way through the answer without sending Newton into a fury.

"She's a woman with detailed information," Richard finally answered.

"So, she's a spy?"

"Technically, she's a courier, but—"

Newton shook his head. "I don't like it."

"You don't have to like it, sir. If she delivers results, what's the problem with that?"

"Have you considered that she might be setting you up?"

Richard nodded. "Of course, but I believe she's telling

the truth. And without her, I'll never come close to finding the cipher in a reasonable amount of time."

"Fine, I'll agree to help her, but you better get moving," Newton said. "If I don't have that cipher in my possession in twenty-four hours, I'm not going to give you a diplomatic visa. Then if you get caught, you'll be on your own. And trust me when I say this, the Japanese are serious rule followers. Your little chapter will be a short one either way if you don't get that device back."

"I'll do my best, sir," Richard said.

"That's not what I want to hear," Newton said. "I want to hear that you'll have it my hands if it's the last thing you do. Understand?"

Richard nodded.

"You're probably going to need this," Newton said as he slapped a stack of cash on the desk. "Now, get going. The clock is ticking."

After Richard grabbed the money, he dumped the letters out onto the desk and then hurried toward the door. He didn't want to be late. Hisako was waiting.

CHAPTER 12

RICHARD PLANNED TO MEET HISAKO FOR LUNCH NEAR the embassy. However, he needed to shake the two detectives following him. Hisako had given him some ideas on how exactly to do that.

Two blocks from the designated restaurant, Richard entered an acupuncture clinic. He was greeted by a doctor in a white robe who introduced himself at Hideyo Tezuka. Richard scanned the waiting area, which was decorated with nature sketches and consisted of three chairs up against the far wall.

"Do you speak English?" Richard asked.

Tezuka, his hair bunched in a tight bun, nodded. "Wait one moment while I prepare your treatment." He motioned for Richard to sit down.

Before Tezuka returned, the two detectives entered the clinic and sat in the empty seats next to Richard. He smiled politely at the men but didn't say anything.

When Tezuka returned, he said something to the men in Japanese before looking at Richard and inviting him to enter the back room. A pair of women smiled at Richard as he entered the treatment area. One tried to take his coat, but he drew back, refusing to allow her to help him.

"I need your help," Richard said. "I'm not really here for acupuncture."

"I know," Tezuka said. "Hisako told me. But we need this to be as realistic as possible if you want this to work."

Tezuka nodded knowingly at the women. One took Richard's coat, while the other directed him to the table. She unbuttoned his shirt and gently leaned him back.

"Please turn over," Tezuka said.

Richard embraced adventure and had heard plenty about this ancient Japanese art, but needles weren't something he was fond of. And when he saw Tezuka grab a fistful of them, Richard's breathing grew shallow.

"You're not going to stick those in me, are you?" he asked as he turned on his side.

Tezuka held up a needle and studied it. "This is what acupuncture is all about. If we're going to make this realistic, I'm going to make you scream. Now, please lie on your stomach."

"Isn't there another way to do this?" Richard asked.

The two women massaged his back while gently pushing him onto his stomach.

"Is this going to hurt, doc?" he asked.

"Of course not," Tezuka said before jamming the first needle into Richard.

He screamed as the first one pierced his skin.

The women giggled, but Richard wasn't amused. "Come on, doc. This isn't necessary."

"Aren't you writing a book on Japan?" Tezuka asked. "Don't you want to tell readers about Japanese traditions?"

"Yes, but I want to live to tell about them," Richard said. "It feels like my entire body is on fire."

"That will soon change," Tezuka said as he guided another needle into Richard's back.

This process continued for several minutes—Tezuka easing a needle into Richard while he begged for the doctor to stop. Eventually, Richard resigned himself to his fate, and strangely enough, the pain dissipated.

After ten minutes, Tezuka pulled up a chair next to the table and crouched down so he could get eye level with Richard.

"How are you feeling?" Tezuka asked.

"Weird, but better," Richard said. "What kind of magic is this?"

"The kind that will heal your entire body," Tezuka said before dropping his voice to a whisper. "I'm going to remove the needles, and I want you to be silent. When I am finished, I will help you up and lead you to our back exit into the alley. These procedures can last as long as an hour, and that should give you more than enough time to escape."

Tezuka then stood and initiated the process of taking out all the needles. When he was finished, Richard felt better, as if the past week of sleeping on hard surfaces or in awkward positions never happened.

"Thanks, doc," Richard said in a hushed tone before handing him a wad of cash three times what Tezuka's hourly posted rate was.

Tezuka smiled. "Good luck," he whispered.

Richard stole into the tight corridor behind the acupuncture office and headed toward the main street. After winding his way through the streets of Tokyo, he entered the designated restaurant and found Hisako sitting in the back corner just as she had promised. And the detectives who'd been tailing Richard were nowhere in sight.

"How was Dr. Tezuka?" she asked.

"Pleasant and painful," Richard said. "He made me undergo acupuncture for authenticity."

"It gets easier the more often you do it."

Richard shook his head. "I'm not sure I want to acquire

such a tolerance for that."

They both ordered and commenced to plotting.

"So, I made a big promise," Richard said. "I told the ambassador at the embassy that I would get the cipher back. Are we still going to be able to do that?"

"If everything goes as planned, it should be a simple mission. First, we find out where it is; then we steal it back."

"That's not a plan. That's a goal."

Hisako nodded. "Sure, but there's not much use in concocting a plan when you don't know where the cipher is. Once we know the location, we'll devise a scheme to steal it."

"And how are we going to find out where it is? I was hoping you already knew."

"Not yet," she said. "But I found out from one of my associates that Prince Naruhiko will host a meeting with several other members of the intelligence branch of the Japanese military. And I received confirmation that they will be discussing the cipher."

"Will it be there?" Richard asked.

Hisako shrugged. "Even if it is, we can't charge into the room and seize it. The men invited tonight will be some of Japan's finest. Without a meticulous plan, we'll be captured or killed. That much I can guarantee."

"What do you want me to do?" Richard asked.

"I'll need your help breaking into the compound where the meeting is scheduled to take place. Once I'm inside, I'll sneak up to the room, listen to the conversation, and report back to you what I learned. Deal?"

"Sure," Richard said. "It's not like there's much of a choice for me. My grasp of the Japanese language is a loose one at best."

"And did you ask the ambassador about granting me my request?"

"He's on board, but we have to get that cipher back in twenty-four hours."

"Twenty-four hour? Are you insane? I hope you didn't promise them that."

Richard winced. "Actually, I did."

"You're crazier than you look."

"We can do it. We'll just have to move quickly."

"If you say so," she said.

Richard smiled and winked at her. "You gotta have a little faith."

* * *

JUST AFTER DARK, Hisako led Richard along a corridor near the heavily guarded compound where Prince Naruhiko held his regular meetings with higher-ups in the Japanese military. She crouched low, staying in the shadows from the streetlamp around the corner of an adjacent building.

"When I tell you go, I need you to boost me as high as you can so I can reach the top of that wall," she said.

"You think you can get up there?" Richard asked.

"It wouldn't be the first time I've scaled a fortress."

"You are aware that if you hadn't stolen that cipher from me, we wouldn't have to be doing this," Richard said.

"You won't let me forget. But why don't we focus on the present?"

Richard nodded. "Just give me the word."

Hisako waited for the two guards near the entrance to turn their attention in the opposite direction. But they didn't, faithfully holding their gaze along the street that ran in front of the building.

"We need a distraction," she said.

"Coming right up," Richard said.

Before she could protest or even ask what he planned to do, Richard hurled two rocks in quick succession toward the other side of the gate. The noise drew the guard's focus.

"Good work," she said. "Let's go."

Hisako and Richard hustled up to the corner of the wall and sprang into action. Backing up a couple strides so she could get momentum, Hisako waited for Richard to form a makeshift step by interlocking his fingers.

"Ready?" he asked.

She nodded before exploding into a sprint. After she stepped on his hand, he thrusted her upward. Hisako rose high enough to get her arms well over the wall, gripping the other side and pulling her body flush up against it. She flashed a thumbs up sign to Richard before hurling herself over the edge. For a moment, she hung by her fingertips and scanned the ground beneath her. Satisfied that she wouldn't be impaled or land on something that would draw the ire of the entire company of men handling security inside, she let go. Her light landing barely made a sound.

She glanced up at the building in the middle of the compound that towered above the ground. With numerous nooks and crannies to stay in the shadows, she went to work wedging her feet in tight spaces opposite of one another.

As she glided up the wall, she couldn't help but think about how easy it was, a far cry from the first time she attempted it under Prince Naruhiko's watchful eye. He'd recruited her a week earlier to serve as a courier before deciding she could be even more useful. But just as she had seen the prince do so many times before with others, he cast her aside, branding her as a traitor.

At least that's what she thought. And she wasn't interested in verifying that information given how she'd seen the prince follow this same path many times before when he was ready to discard someone.

Hisako shimmied up to the ledge just beneath the

window. A fire crackled across the room, making it a little more difficult to hear the conversation. She peered through the slats in the window, taking account of all the officials in the room: two military commanders as well as Prince Naruhiko and three other intelligence officers.

"Gentlemen, thank you for joining me tonight," Naruhiko said in Japanese. "I appreciate everyone taking the time to be here for this emergency discussion. We have a problem, and we need to act quickly."

"A few days ago, one of our spies retrieved this from an American on a ship crossing between Russia and Japan," he continued.

Hisako couldn't see the object since she remained out of sight, but she knew exactly what he was talking about, even if he did so only in vague generalities. As she tried to remain in position, she felt her calf muscles burning.

"Unfortunately, we've made the determination that this object has likely been replicated many times over and it would be in our best interest to create a new cipher to distribute and retire this one."

"This isn't an easy process," one of the commanders said.

"Of course not," Naruhiko said. "However, I had the foresight to order the monks at Taiseki-ji to begin crafting us a new one several weeks ago, the moment I learned our cipher had been compromised."

"Any idea when it will be ready?" an intelligence officer asked. "We can't delay in deploying a new code or else our entire communication will be hampered."

"I'm going to go to Taiseki-ji's hidden temple first thing in the morning to see what I can learn," Naruhiko said.

Armed with all the information she needed, she slid down the wall and then hustled across the courtyard to where she first came over where Richard had left a rope for her. Tossing it over the side, she waited until she felt a tug, signaling that he was in place. Then she tied it around her waist and climbed up and over.

Once she reached the other side, she detached from the line and hustled down an alley with Richard. When they stopped, he bombarded her with questions.

"What'd you find out?" he asked. "Was the cipher with them? Can we get the device back tonight?"

Hisako caught her breath and sat down. "It's not good."

"What do you mean?"

"The prince is going to Taiseki-ji's secret monastery to retrieve a new cipher that's being built and will be deployed to all the spies," she said.

Richard furrowed his brow. "Taiseki-ji?"

"Yes, it's an ancient Buddhist temple in the foothills of Mt. Fuji."

"And what's so bad about that?"

"The monks who have helped create the cipher live in a secret temple on Mt. Fuji, closer to the peak."

"And how's that a problem?" he asked.

"It's a treacherous journey."

"Then how is the prince going to make it?" Richard asked.

"There are locals who will help him because he's the prince, but you're not a native."

Richard shook his head. "I can still do it."

"It's a mission destined to end in failure."

A wry smile spread across Richard's face. "Those are my favorite kind."

CHAPTER 13

RICHARD RUBBED HIS EYES IN AN EFFORT TO DIMINISH the sagging bags caused from a lack of sleep as he strode up to the gates of the American consulate. Aside from already being tired, he could hardly sleep after Hisako relayed what she learned at Prince Naruhiko's secret intelligence meeting. Richard was going to get the opportunity to climb Mt. Fuji, even if it was perilous or even foolish, according to Hisako.

Harold Newton sat on the porch that extended the width of the building, puffing on a cigar and rocking in a chair.

"Is this how you deal with being homesick?" Richard asked.

Newton stood and shuffled over toward Richard. "What do you mean?"

"Don't you have big porches in Mississippi, just like we do in Tennessee?"

"How did you know that's where I was from?"

"I'm in intelligence, sir. Information is my lifeblood."

Newton grunted. "Right now, your lifeline depends on whether or not you got that cipher back last night."

Richard sucked a breath through his teeth. "It didn't go exactly like we thought it would."

"Then how did it go?" Newton asked.

Richard relayed all the important discussion points Hisako had passed along, including the most rage-inducing nugget about the cipher. Mouth agape, Newton stared at Richard.

"What do you mean the Japanese don't intend to use the cipher anymore?" Newton asked. "How are they going to communicate?"

"They're building a new cipher."

Newton removed the cigar from his mouth. "Building one?"

"According to Hisako, a group of Buddhist monks aid the Japanese intelligence department. And the prince announced that he tasked them to work on this urgent project weeks ago. He's heading up to a secret monastery today to check on the project."

"What temple is that?" Newton asked.

"Taiseki-ji," Richard said. "Or rather, Taiseki-ji's hidden temple. They have a team of master craftsmen who create the cipher from wood who live in the mountain. It's fascinating from what I understand."

Newton puffed on his cigar and slapped Richard on the back. "Well, son, we're not here to marvel at trinkets a bunch of monks can whip up, especially if it means they pose a threat to our country's security. Now, I need you to do your best to go get that cipher for Uncle Sam. And if you fail, it's on you. If you hadn't lost the thing in the first place, we wouldn't be in this situation."

"I'm aware of how we got here, sir," Richard said. "I should've kept my guard up. But the truth is we have an extraordinary opportunity to steal their cipher before it even reaches offices worldwide."

"That's a big if," Newton said. "You have to go get it—and not get caught."

Richard took a deep breath and exhaled slowly. "I'm going to make you proud, sir. But there's just one thing I need."

"And what's that?"

"I need help from someone who knows how to navigate the mountain."

Newton glanced at Ford, who'd just arrived in time to hear the last minute of the conversation.

"Are you thinking what I'm thinking?" Ford asked.

Newton nodded. "Get him Thomas's information. If anyone can help, he can."

Ford scurried off and returned moments later with a piece of paper that had an address scrawled on it.

"Mr. Thomas Orde-Lees," Richard read aloud. "Friend of yours?"

Newton closed one eye and looked skyward, as if searching for how to answer the question. "More like a helpful contact. He's former British military and has been willing to help us on occasion."

"But if you're going to get him to help you, you're going to need this as well," Ford said before tossing a stack of cash to Richard.

"How much is in here?" he asked as he flipped his thumb along the edge of the bills.

"Two grand," Ford said. "That should be enough to get him to help you. But if he'll do it for less, that would be even better."

"And what kind of temperament does this Mr. Lees have?" Richard asked.

Newton chuckled. "Go see for yourself."

* * *

RICHARD RENDEZVOUSED with Hisako as they went together to the address listed for Thomas Orde-Lees. After a short walk, they approached the steps of the British Embassy.

"You didn't tell me we were going to visit a diplomat," Hisako said.

"If I knew that, I would've told you," Richard said. "Everyone seemed reluctant to tell me the truth about this man. So, I guess we'll find out about him together."

A guard ushered them onto the grounds before escorting them to Thomas Orde-Lees's office. He knocked on the door, which flew open. A man with an aviator hat and a cigarette dangling from his lips greeted them with a sneer before walking away without inviting them in. However, he left the door open, an invitation Richard seized.

"May we come in, sir?" he asked.

Lees looked over his shoulder and waved the duo inside. "Might as well see what you came here for."

He stroked his goatee while studying the parachute spread out across the floor, refusing to initiate any conversation with the visitors. Falling to his knees, he folded the material back and forth while mumbling to himself.

"Sir, did we come at a bad time?" Richard asked.

"No, of course not," Lees said in his thick English accent. "But I am rather busy at the moment. Perhaps you can come back later."

Richard shook his head. "I'm afraid this can't wait."

"Well, you better jolly well get on with it before I strap this parachute to your back and throw you off the tallest pagoda I can find," Lees said.

Richard caught himself staring at a picture of Lees standing on the deck of a ship. "You sailed with Sir Shackleton on the Endurance?"

Lees pulled the cigarette out of his mouth as he looked up at Richard. "Do you want my autograph or did you come here for something else? Because I really don't have time for games, lad."

"I need help climbing Mt. Fuji," Richard said.

Lees chuckled as he continued folding the parachute. After he stopped, he looked up at Richard.

"Oh, you're serious," Lees said. "I thought you were being funny."

"I'm very serious."

"In that case, you're a nutter."

"A what?" Richard asked.

"He thinks you're crazy," Hisako whispered.

Lees stood and stared at Richard for a moment. "You appear to be a sane chap, but anyone who wants to climb Mt. Fuji this time of year has some mental deficiencies."

"It doesn't look impossible."

"There's a reason why even the locals don't attempt to climb Mt. Fuji during the winter."

Richard shrugged. "I don't have much choice."

"Is someone forcing you to do this?"

"No, but—"

"Then you can wait."

Richard shook his head. "Actually, it can't."

Lees took another long drag on his cigarette. "Who told you about me?"

"Harold Newton from the U.S. consulate."

"Oh, blimey. Another spy," he said, falling back to his knees again to work with the parachute.

"The Japanese are building a cipher in a monastery up Mt. Fuji, and I need to get my hands on it before they circulate it."

"If you steal it, that won't do you any good," Lees said.

"That's why I'm going to take pictures of it so we can duplicate it."

Lees nodded. "I had a friend who was murdered by a Japanese spy. So, I'll help you. But you must know that this will be a treacherous expedition. The wind, the ice, the sudden storms that can appear around Mt. Fuji—it's unlike anything you've probably ever seen."

"Have you ever attempted to summit Mt. Fuji this time of year?" Hisako asked.

"Once," Lees said as he snuffed out his cigarette in the ashtray on his desk. "Let's just say things didn't go well. That's why I'm trying to dissuade you."

"If it wasn't so urgent, I might exercise some restraint," Richard said. "But that's not a luxury I have right now."

"Then come with me," Lees said. "I'll get you everything you need but luck. Because if you're going to survive up there, you're going to need more than just the right equipment."

Lees marched across the room and opened up a closet packed with ropes, spiked boots, winter coats, tents, lanterns, and walking sticks. But the first thing Lees grabbed was an axe.

"If all else fails, swing this," Lees said. "It's the most important tool you'll take with you."

"More so than a rope?" Richard asked.

Lees nodded. "A rope won't help you when you're falling down the side of a mountain."

After a few minutes, Lees finished stuffing a backpack for Richard and then handed it to him.

"Wish me luck," Richard said.

"Like I said, you'll need more than that," Lees said. "You'll need the climb of your life."

Richard cinched the straps down on his shoulders and smiled.

Mt. Fuji awaits!

CHAPTER 14

RICHARD AND HISAKO ARRANGED TRANSPORTATION TO get closer to the base of Mt. Fuji after collecting all the supplies from Lees. And by dawn the next morning, Richard struck off for Taiseki-ji's secret monastery with Hisako. She had agreed to accompany him for a short distance before turning back.

Between the howling wind and the snow crunching beneath their feet, conversation was a struggle. They walked for a few minutes along the banks of Lake Shoji before taking cover in a cluster of trees.

"Don't forget what I told you," Hisako said. "But if you do—"

"Relax," Richard said. "I can bluff my way through anything."

"These aren't the kind of people who will forgive you just because you can make them laugh. Take everything very seriously."

"I will," Richard said. "And if I'm successful, this trip could be historic."

She smiled. "That's what you're hoping for, isn't it?"

"I admit it'd be nice to be part of something like that. But if not, the adventure will be satisfying enough. Just stay out of sight until I get back. Once I capture the cipher, we'll talk with Newton about how to help you escape Naruhiko's death sentence."

"I'll be waiting."

Richard gave her a hug before turning toward the mountain and continuing his hike.

For the next hour, he worked his way through a grove of cypress trees. The wintry mix pelting him combined with the slick conditions on the ground resulted in slow plodding. If it had been possible, Richard would have sprinted through the forest and raced to the top. But the weather didn't afford him any such opportunity. Instead, he methodically picked his way through the woods before reaching a clearing near the base of Mt. Fuji.

A light snow started to fall on the already icy ground. He dug his boots into the fresh powder and began to climb up the slow incline. According to Hisako, the climb up to Taiseki-ji's secret monastery would take around three hours, depending on the conditions. As much as Richard wanted to reach the temple faster, he realized that his journey was likely to take much longer. The slick surface coupled with the windier conditions higher up the slope meant he needed to exercise extreme caution.

After a half-hour, he ventured above the tree line, increasing his degree of difficulty. The flat light created even more challenges, making the contours of the rock almost impossible to see. More than once, Richard slipped after thinking he'd secured his footing but dug into the ice to stop the slide.

As Richard continued to work his way toward the monastery, he remembered the date and tried to keep his composure. It was five years to the day that Richard's life was turned upside down when his brother Wesley died suddenly from a short bout with rheumatic fever. He was only fourteen and had plenty of life ahead of him.

Wesley's death was the driving force behind Richard

doing his best to turn his favorite phrase from Latin class—carpe diem—into a mantra for how to spend the rest of his life. Four years Richard's junior, Wesley was a bundle of energy, fearless in so many respects. He embraced challenges, charging into them without any concern as to what might happen should he fail. Even as he was battling the illness that eventually took his life, Wesley wrote Richard a letter regarding plans to travel to California together to see the Pacific coast. He intended to go there soon to honor his brother's wishes, but Richard decided the best way to remember his brother would be to live life to the fullest, never having any regrets. At least, any more regrets. Richard already shouldered the burden of lamenting how he should've spent more time with Wesley. But that was in the past now, unable to be altered. However, Richard fully intended to move forward in a way that would make Wesley proud.

Richard pressed through the freezing temperatures as he continued his slow ascent. After another ten minutes, he reached a small relief in the mountain, enabling him to take a short break. Richard sat on his haunches while gulping down some tea Hisako had given him in a thermos. He found the drink soothing, using the respite to plot his way up to the spot Hisako pointed out was the way into the secret monastery. The nook seemed small while he was at the base, but it was substantially larger than he first thought. From Richard's perspective, he still didn't think it was more than five feet tall and less than a meter wide. But it didn't appear nearly as tight as it did earlier in his climb.

Rested and ready, Richard repacked his thermos and continued his climb. He had barely put on all his gear again before he slipped on the ice. Falling face first, he started sliding down the slight incline. He attempted to dig his spikes into the ground but couldn't get them in deep enough. He continued to drift toward the edge, which was a dramatic drop down a sheer cliff face.

Richard's backpack pulled him to the side, inhibiting his ability to take control of the situation. He reached for his pickaxe while still heading feet first toward a plunge to sure death. Relentlessly trying to slam his shoes into the ice, he fumbled for his pickaxe. When he pulled on it, he noticed the loop had twisted, preventing him from yanking the tool free. He worked furiously to rip it out before it was too late.

He took a quick peek below to see he was rapidly running out of room. With one last gasp, he jerked the handle free from his pack and wielded the device, slamming the point into the ice. At first, it didn't do much and he continued sliding. However, just as his legs slid over the edge, the blade caught on a rock, halting Richard's descent as his legs dangled over the side.

After taking a deep breath for composure, Richard carefully pulled himself to the solid surface and walked gingerly back up the slope toward the rock face. He adjusted his pack then wrapped his hands around the axe handle.

But before he could make another move, he heard the sound of ice crunching beneath feet behind him.

Richard spun around to see a half-dozen men dressed in Samurai garb pointing their swords at him. He threw his hands in the air as the men fanned out in a semicircle around him.

"Can I help you with anything?" Richard said.

One of the men nodded as he stepped forward. "An American?"

Richard nodded. "I hope that isn't a problem for you gentlemen."

"Depends," the man said as he waved his weapon back and forth.

"On what?"

"How badly you want to continue climbing Mt. Fuji."

Richard shook his head. "I'm sorry, but I don't want to give off the wrong impression. I'm not here to intrude on your territory. I just—"

The leader laughed heartily before the other warriors joined him.

Richard watched wide-eyed at their display of amusement. "What? What did I say?"

"You will only do what we tell you to, or you will die," the leader said. "Is that clear?"

"Of course, sir. I merely wanted to say that—"

"Silence. We don't want to hear your explanation or your excuses."

"Then what do you want?" Richard asked.

"Payment for your passage."

"I'm afraid I didn't bring a large sum of money with me on this journey," Richard said. "I was trying to pack light to make my climb more enjoyable."

"Are you enjoying things right now?"

Richard shook his head. "Things could be better."

"Of course they could. And you're going to make them better for us."

"And how am I going to do that?"

"You're going to kill someone for us."

"Kill someone?" Richard asked. "I'm not a murderer for hire."

The leader paced in front of Richard. "What is your name?"

"Richard Halliburton."

"All right, Mr. Halliburton, how much do you value your own life?"

"I rather enjoy being alive," Richard said, cracking a

smile in hopes that levity might soften the hardened man.

"If that's true, you'll murder the man I'm assigning you to kill."

"And if I don't?" Richard asked.

"When you come back down the mountain, I'll murder you in his place."

CHAPTER 15

RICHARD SWALLOWED HARD AS HIS GAZE SHIFTED between the samurai warrior and the edge of the blade that appeared to get closer with each statement he made. He turned the blade sideways and used the flat portion to lift Richard's chin.

"I've thought about it," Richard said, "and I've had a change of heart. I'll agree to do your favor."

The man lowered his blade as a smile spread across his face. "Finally, an American I like."

Richard sighed but remained uneasy, despite the lightened mood.

"My name is Hattori Mitsunari," the warrior said as he slid his weapon through his belt. "And I'm the leader of the only active order of samurais still operating."

"I thought samurais were a thing of the past," Richard said, feeling more relaxed with each passing moment.

"Technically, we don't exist. But we are all direct descendants from other warriors who have walked these same hallowed grounds on Mt. Fuji," Mitsunari said. "Despite what the leaders of today want, we will not go away quietly. And they know better than to try and banish us. Japan was built on legend and has an ancient past that can't be ignored. It's part of who we are."

Richard nodded. "I understand you want to continue

to practice your art, but—"

"Being a samurai isn't an art. It is a way of life."

"My apologies," Richard said. "I understand you want to continue your way of life, but is it necessary to murder someone?"

"You have no idea what that traitor has done to us," Mitsunari said as he glanced around at his men who were nodding. He said something in Japanese, and they all joined him in the gesture.

"What did he do that warrants a death sentence?"

"Bhodi Daido used to be a samurai," Mitsunari said. "He was fierce and loyal. But something happened: his brother died. Instead of turning his pain into becoming a greater warrior, he turned to Buddhism."

"We all deal with grief differently," Richard said.

"Part of the samurai code is that we allow our fellow warriors to grieve. That was never the problem. It was how he decided to impose his newly discovered religion on all of us."

Richard furrowed his brow. "Bhodi became a monk?"

"Not only did he turn to the monastery, he decided that the way of the samurai needed to cease. The Japanese government had stated that samurais no longer existed, but only as a way to calm fears that our country was too savage to visit. However, many people who visit Japan want to see samurais, so the authorities never enforced the laws banning us."

"But Bhodi didn't see it that way, did he?" Richard asked.

Mitsunari shook his head. "Bhodi thought every samurai needed to be outed. He met a reporter who was hiking up Mt. Fuji and told him where our secret Mt. Fuji hideout was. Once that news went public, hikers left trail and invaded our den. After a couple weeks of pressure from organizations all over the world to make Japan safer for tourists, the government seized our hideout."

"Yet, here you are," Richard said.

"Don't mistake our presence for the process being easy," Mitsunari said. "We have all endured great hardship to maintain the samurai way. While I don't care if Bhodi decided to turn his back on his brothers, we will not allow such an act that threatened to eliminate us altogether go unpunished."

Richard eyed Mitsunari carefully. "But with death? Is that a just punishment?"

"He knows what he did and how harmful it was. There is no better alternative."

Richard shrugged. "Apparently I don't have much of a choice, but I want you to know that I'm not fond of this idea."

"Complete the task, and you will be allowed to go free," Mitsunari said. "Should you fail, you will die in his place."

Richard took a deep breath and put his hands on his hips. "I'm glad we could establish the ground rules. Anything else I need to know?"

"I want proof that he's dead," Mitsunari said.

"His head, perhaps," Richard suggested.

"I'll settle for an ear."

"An ear it is," Richard said.

Mitsunari eyed Richard closely. "We'll anxiously await your return."

Richard gathered his belongings and turned toward the rock face behind him. He swung his pickaxe into the ice before tugging on the handle to make sure the tool was secure. Satisfied that he could proceed, he resumed his ascent. Twenty minutes later, he looked back over his shoulder where he'd met the samurais. They were gone.

Richard plodded along for the next hour until he neared the space that Hisako had identified as the entrance to the monastery. A short plateau allowed him to rest for a few minutes before approaching the opening in the mountain.

The sky grew dark and the wind picked up, blowing twice as hard as it had near the base. Richard headed toward the opening, unsure of what he might do if he was denied access.

The small entrance into the mountain seemed so natural that Richard hardly believed the monks carved it out of the rock as Hisako had explained. He cautiously ventured inside. The narrow opening felt more like a maze, weaving back and forth in a series of sharp turns. However, when Richard reached a small clearing, he noticed a large wall lit by a series of torches positioned along the outside. He couldn't help but enjoy the warmth provided by Mt. Fuji's interior, heated by a scant measure of volcanic activity deep below the surface. With the mountain's last eruption occurring more than 200 years ago, scientists remained confident that Mt. Fuji wasn't in danger of erupting again any time soon.

Richard heard monks chanting behind the wall, affirming that he was in the right place. He strode up to the door and knocked. Eventually a man slid open a small portal and peered outside. He said something in Japanese, but Richard didn't understand.

"Can you help me?" Richard asked.

The man scowled and shook his head.

"Do you not understand me, or are you telling me no?"

"What do you want?" the man asked.

"Bhodi Daido," Richard said. "Do you know him?"

"Bhodi?" the man asked.

Richard nodded. The slit was slammed shut as Richard heard the pitter-patter of feet racing away from the entrance.

After what felt like several minutes, the door swung open and a man armed with a sword joined Richard beyond the gates.

"You speak English," Bhodi said.

"Yes, I apologize, but my Japanese is rather weak, nearly non-existent."

"Non-existent?" Bhodi asked.

"Oh, never mind," Richard said. "I came to talk to you about the samurai warriors down the mountain. Are you familiar with them?"

Bhodi shrugged. "Who's asking?"

"I'm sorry, but my name is Richard Halliburton, and I'm an American visiting Japan for a magazine article I'm writing."

"And you want to speak with me?"

Richard eyed the dagger in Bhodi's hand. "Can you please put that away? I'm not here to attack you. In fact, I'm here for just the opposite. I'm here to save you."

Bhodi chuckled. "I can handle myself. Now if you came all the way up here to tell me that, I suggest you turn around and leave."

"I thought that's what you'd say," Richard said. "That's what any samurai warrior would say."

Bhodi narrowed his eyes "Who are you really?"

"I told you. I'm an adventure writer, working on an article on Mt. Fuji. And on my way up the mountain, I was detained by a small group of samurai warriors that are very upset with you for exposing their hideout."

"It's an antiquated art form that needs to be stopped. They would still be killing and plundering their neighbors' land if given the opportunity."

"While I agree with your sentiments, the leader of the group looked very intent on killing you."

Bhodi shrugged. "And how are you going to change

that? Don't you think I already have a good idea that they want to kill me?"

"Sure, but—"

"What do you really want?"

Richard interlocked his fingers and drew them close to his chest in a prayerful gesture. "Please, hear me out. I think we can work together to end this threat, satisfying their need for revenge while allowing you to go about the rest of your life without the fear that someone behind you might be swinging a blade aimed for your neck."

"I'm listening."

"They are requiring me to bring your ear as proof that I've killed you."

Bhodi raised his dagger. "If you think I'm going to cut off my ear—"

"No, no. Of course not. I'll give him one from someone who is already dead."

"Do you have a dead body? Because everyone who dies up here is cremated."

Richard furrowed his brow. "I hear that the monks up here are master craftsmen. Perhaps, they can make one?"

"Make an ear?"

Richard nodded.

"I suppose it's possible. But then I'd have to explain my background as a former samurai warrior. I'm not sure I'd be welcome here anymore if the monks learned what I used to do. You don't have any other ideas, do you?"

Richard stroked his chin. "Do you happen to have any other dead bodies?"

"Wait a minute. There was a monk who died last week who specifically asked to be buried. His body is in a sealed casket. But if you can get to it somehow . . ."

"That was the other half of my proposal," Richard said.

"I need entrance into the monastery."

"For your article? The monks aren't fond of anyone writing about them."

Richard shook his head. "For my own personal enlightenment. I want to experience what goes on here and see if I can glean anything from it."

"That plan might work, but I can't just let you in," Bhodi said. "I need to bring one of our priests here. There's only one who speaks English. Please wait right here, and I'll return soon."

Richard paced while he waited outside the gates for Bhodi's return. After a few minutes, he emerged from behind the door, leading a priest with him.

The priest introduced himself as Saicho.

"It's a pleasure to meet you," Richard said before bowing.

"What can I help you with, my child?"

"I want to spend a few days here and was wondering if I could experience Buddhism with you and the other monks here."

"We don't allow tourists in here, especially cameras," Saicho said, glancing at Richard's camera that was hanging out of his bag.

"None of this is important to me," Richard said. "I want to find a path to greater enlightenment, and I believe that you can show me the way there."

"I appreciate your zeal, but I'm afraid at this time we cannot allow you access to our hallowed and holy grounds. I hope you'll find what you're looking for."

Before Richard could respond, a bird swooped in, dipping and diving erratically. Richard ducked as the animal swiped him on top of his head while chattering loudly.

"Now look," the priest said. "A sign to confirm my decision."

"Wait," Richard said. "Is that it? You're just going to reject me like that? No appeal? No second chance? You saw a bird and that's it?"

Saicho shook his head. "I have spoken." After issuing his judgment, he turned and walked back inside the gates.

"I'm sorry," Bhodi mouthed to Richard while closing off the entrance.

"So what am I supposed to do now?" Richard called.

Moments later, the door opened again and the original guard appeared. "I don't know what you're supposed to do, but you're going to need to do it outside."

"Are you insane? I can't make that descent in the dark? You'd be sending me to my death."

The guard shrugged. "I don't make the rules. I only enforce them."

"Look, I'll leave first thing in the morning, but you can't make me stay out there. I'll either freeze to death or die on my way down."

"Maybe you should've considered that before you came up here," the guard said before locking the gate.

Richard took a deep breath and then exhaled slowly. He wasn't sure if the monastery guards would physically remove him, but he wasn't interested in knowing that definitively.

There has to be another way.

The bird that had flown near Richard was squawking and continued to dip and dive before slamming into a nearby boulder.

Richard rushed over to the animal, scooping it up. The bird's head bobbled as its eyes opened slowly and then closed, repeating that several times before its eyes remained closed. Richard enveloped the animal in his hands, testing for a pulse. Its heart was still beating.

"I know how you feel," Richard said. "That about sums up my day."

"Outside now," the other guard from behind the wall shouted.

Richard growled as he rose to his feet to follow the edict. He wound his way through the maze-like entrance until he stepped into the bitter winds blasting across the side of the mountain. Leaning back against the rock, Richard tucked the bird in his coat and remained just inside the entrance to avoid the wind.

"What are they going to do to us, little fellow?" Richard asked his new friend. "I promise I won't be as cruel as these men."

Richard's teeth chattered as he tried to keep himself warm. He stared out into the stormy scene as daylight had all but faded, yielding to dark-gray skies. In a matter of minutes, night would fall, and Richard wasn't sure he'd be able to survive if he was forced into the open.

"How are you doing in there? Staying warm?" Richard asked. "Good. That makes one of us."

Richard remained still as he heard the shuffling of feet drawing closer. He braced for the worst as he looked in the direction of the footfalls.

Then Saicho emerged around the corner, his face solemn and hands clasped in front of him.

"I thought we instructed you to move outside," he said.

Richard bit his lip as he rose to his feet and trudged toward the opening.

CHAPTER 16

RICHARD SHOOK HIS HEAD AS HE GLANCED BACK AT the priest. The old man hadn't moved as he eyed Richard shuffling off into the night. But Richard stopped, spinning on his heels and marching back toward the man.

"Before I go, I just need to say one thing," Richard said. "And it's this—"

"Quiet, my child," Saicho said. "I'm not here to send you into the cold darkness. I'm here to invite you into the warm light."

"Invite me in?" Richard asked, his eyes widening. "Did you hear that, little guy? They're going to let us inside."

"Come now. I know you're freezing."

Richard scrambled to his feet, continuing to shield the bird from the elements. He flung his pack over his shoulder and followed the priest.

"If you don't mind me asking, what made you change your mind?" Richard asked.

The priest placed his hands behind his back as he walked. "You showed pity to a helpless animal. That's all I need to know about what kind of man you are."

Richard chuckled and shook his head. "One moment doesn't make a man."

"And what does make a man?" Saicho asked.

"The sum of our decisions in both our strongest and weakest moments is what determines what kind of person we become," Richard said. "It displays the type of character we have."

Saicho nodded. "And in a time of great weakness, you chose to show pity toward a bird. I don't think I'll regret allowing you inside for a night."

"Or two?" Richard asked. "Or maybe five or six?"

"We'll see. Just don't make me regret my decision."

"I'll make you proud," Richard said, hustling to keep pace with the elderly man who seemed to glide across the ground.

"The goal is not to make me proud but to be true to yourself," Saicho said.

"I'm not sure what that means, but my grandmother used to always tell me to be authentic. And that's what I try to do."

"Are you always successful in that endeavor?"

Richard huffed a soft laugh through his nose. "Is that even possible?"

"When you become enlightened, you will find that every decision you make will enable you to be true to yourself."

"Are you enlightened?" Richard asked.

"One day, my child, one day."

But Richard already knew the answer to that question based on Saicho's definition of the word.

An enlightened person wouldn't force a weary traveler into the snow to spend the night.

"Perhaps you're more enlightened than me," Saicho said.

Richard stopped and eyed the priest. "What did you say?"

Saicho kept walking. "I know what you were thinking."

"Was that some kind of Buddhist magic trick?" Richard asked.

"No magic involved. Your thoughts were simply written all over your face."

Richard resumed following Saicho. "I'm not sure Buddhism is for me."

"If your mind is open, it can be changed."

"Who said that? One of your revered leaders?"

Saicho grunted. "Not everything we say is from our religion. Some things just make common sense."

As they entered the gates, Richard took in the surprising beauty of a temple tucked away in the side of a mountain. The monks had utilized natural features of the cave like boulders and tunnels and incorporated them into the sprawling sanctuary. Richard stayed close behind Saicho, who maneuvered through the other monks working in silence. Upon reaching a small room with a counter and rows of books, Saicho told Richard to sit at one of the desks in the corner and that someone would be with him shortly. Then Saicho vanished, leaving through a doorway in the corner.

Richard sat down and absorbed the moment, relaxing for the first time that day. Everything he'd done had been performed at a frenetic pace, the kind necessary to reach the monastery's opening before nightfall. And here he was, deep within the mountain, wondering how he was ever going to locate the cipher and photograph it without getting caught.

Putting the task out of his mind, Richard attempted to enjoy the moment of being able to experience such a rare treat. While the religious element didn't interest him much, the devotion the monks displayed to an ancient tradition was something he wanted to explore. He loved his own country, and the excitement of creating fresh traditions and blazing new trails appealed to his sense of adventure. But there was something about a practice steeped in hundreds of years of history that intrigued him, too.

A few minutes later, Saicho returned with another monk.

"Mr. Halliburton, I apologize for the delay," Saicho said. "Our English speakers here are limited, but I found someone who can teach you our ways for the next few days. Hopefully he will be able to answer all your questions."

"Thank you," Richard said. "I appreciate your help."

"Then may I introduce to you, Ito?" Saicho said before exiting the room

Ito bowed, an action Richard mimicked before being handed a robe.

"My own robe," Richard said as he held it out. "How exciting. Is there a reason for this?"

Ito nodded. "The more we look the same, the more we can focus on enlightenment. Our minds are easily distracted by petty things."

Ito turned his back, allowing Richard to change. When finished, he twirled around.

"How do I look?" Richard asked.

"Like everyone else," Ito said. "Now, come. We have chores to do before dinner."

"Chores?" Richard asked. "Are you aware that I just climbed Mt. Fuji today? I'd rather relax."

"If you don't help, you don't eat," Ito said. "This is not a holiday. If you are to stay here, you must participate like all the other monks. That is a steadfast rule."

Richard shrugged as he nestled the bird into his jacket on his bed. "I guess it could be worse. I could be sleeping outside."

Ito led Richard to a small room. When the door

opened, Richard staggered backward, overcome by the rancid odor emanating from inside.

"What is this place?" he asked, fanning away the air in front of his nose.

Ito smiled and chuckled. "Even monks have to poop."

For the next half hour, Richard struggled as he and Ito cleaned the latrines by removing the waste in buckets. The process seemed to crawl along.

This isn't how I expected the day to end.

After completing the task, Ito and Richard washed up before the evening meal. Dinner was served in silence, which made it difficult to gather more information for his article, much less learn who the special craftsmen designing and creating the cipher were.

And there was one more question that plagued Richard: Where was Prince Naruhiko?

* * *

THE NEXT TWO DAYS were rather torturous. Being outside in nature was almost as important as breathing. He had to be exploring new worlds, taking new adventures, reveling in new experiences. Sloshing floors with water and scrubbing them with a brush wasn't exactly the experience he wanted. And while the monks often ventured outside just before daybreak or during dusk, the nasty winter weather kept Richard from enjoying a scenic view from halfway up Mt. Fuji. His time in the monastery was suffocating, making him antsy to escape.

On the third evening after dinner, Saicho approached Richard. "How are you enjoying your time here?"

"It's certainly not what I expected," Richard said.

"What did you expect?"

"I guess I thought there would be more chanting and focus on some sort of holy scriptures, not hours upon hours of internal reflection."

Saicho chuckled. "This isn't an order of Jesuits. Perhaps your expectations were skewed because you didn't understand that not all monasteries work the same way."

"That's a good assessment of the situation."

"Are you ready to leave?"

"Not yet," Richard said, searching for the right words to tickle Saicho's ears. "I feel as though I'm just starting to connect with myself."

Saicho's eyes brightened. "Then you're on your way, my child. Keep walking that path."

Richard forced a smile, one he held until Saicho turned his back. With only an hour before bedtime, Richard needed to find Bhodi. After a short search, the former samurai was found near the front gate.

"Still watching out for vagrants who wander up the mountain?" Richard asked.

Bhodi turned to face Richard. "You were the first person to walk through those doors in five years. I'm sure my fellow guard barely remembered how to handle the situation. The easiest and most popular trails to the summit are on the other side of the mountain. Only fools come this way."

Richard held up his right hand. "Guilty as charged."

"How has your time here been?"

"In a word: dreary," Richard said. "But I'm adjusting. Meanwhile, I was wondering if you've been able to get that thing we were talking about."

Bhodi nodded. "I'll bring it back to your room tonight just before lights are out."

"Excellent," Richard said. "One more thing."

"What is it?"

"Do you know where the craftsmen are? I want to speak with them about an idea I have."

Bhodi furrowed his brow. "I don't think it works like

that. The craftsmen work on specially commissioned projects."

"Who commissions them?"

"Other priests within the order, I suppose. Unfortunately, these monasteries don't support themselves. We have to have a means for making a sufficient amount of money to keep up this way of life."

Richard sighed. "That's the last group of people I needed to talk to in order to finish my story."

"Ask around. I'm sure someone else can help you."

"The only problem I have with that is most people don't speak my language, and the monk assigned to me isn't very helpful."

"Are you working with Ito?" Bhodi asked.

"How'd you guess?"

Bhodi laughed. "He's not exactly the friendliest person you'll ever meet, and I wouldn't consider him the best at conversation. I used to work as a translator for the British embassy before I joined the order here. It had been so long since I spoke in English I was beginning to wonder if I'd forgotten the language."

Richard nodded. "Thanks for the tip. I'll see what I can find out about the craftsmen."

"Good luck," Bhodi said. "You'll need it."

Richard wandered down the hallway toward the common area, searching for any clues that could lead him to the craftsmen hall. After three days of searching, he was beginning to wonder if the craftsmen were mythic and Hisako had been running a con on him.

He was about to give up and return to his room when a door was flung open, one he hadn't noticed before. But that wasn't surprising, since it appeared to be made out of rock and blended in with the rest of the wall. Inside, several men sat around a table, including three men wearing suits.

Why would they need to have a secret passageway within their own monastery?

Richard tried to act like he didn't pay any attention to it, but his final glance met with the eyes of a monk scrambling to pull the door shut. He scowled at Richard before disappearing.

At least I know it's not a myth.

Richard retired to his room for the night, inspired anew on how to gain access to the hidden room. And he needed to figure it out quickly before he wore out his welcome.

CHAPTER 17

WHEN RICHARD AROSE THE NEXT MORNING AND headed to breakfast, Saicho was waiting in the hallway. He twirled a beaded necklace around his fingers before putting a hand to Richard's chest.

"We need to talk, Mr. Halliburton," Saicho said before guiding Richard out of the flow of traffic.

Other monks quietly maneuvered around the two men until they reached a corner.

"Good morning," Richard said. "Another lovely day here."

"I'm glad you're enjoying your time here, but I came to inform you that it'll be your last," Saicho said. "The council convened last night, and the majority of the members feel as if you've been a distraction, preventing others in their quest for personal enlightenment. And as you know, that is our primary purpose here."

Richard nodded. "I understand. Was it something I did? Something I said?"

"Not at all. We just like to maintain a certain balance within the monastery, and some priests have felt a disturbance."

"Well, I certainly don't want to be thought of as intrusive," Richard said. "I just wanted to capture the essence of what you do here and how Japanese Buddhist monks exist."

"I'm sure you have more than enough by now for any book or magazine article you want to write," Saicho said. "And that's why you'll be leaving in the morning after this winter storm passes. It'll be easier for you to navigate down on a sheet of fresh snow rather than solid ice, which is what will happen after the sun starts to melt all the precipitation we've had the past few days and then it refreezes."

Richard nodded. "I trust your judgment. It's truly been an honor to live here for the past few days."

"You've been a joy to host, my child," Saicho said, placing his hand on top of Richard's head. "I hope this part of your journey leads you to find your own enlightenment."

Richard placed his hands together in a prayer-like posture and bowed his head. Saicho returned the gesture before shuffling toward the dining hall.

When he was gone, Richard entered his room and sat down on his bed to think for a minute. There wasn't much time left now. He still hadn't seen the first room full of craftsmen or Prince Naruhiko either. But Richard was convinced they were still there—and he didn't believe Saicho's reason for requesting an early departure.

* * *

AFTER LUNCH, Richard asked Ito what their evening chore was.

"Your favorite," Ito said. "We'll be cleaning out the latrines."

"It's my last night here," Richard said. "And I'd like to bless you for your kindness and handle that chore on my own."

Ito laughed. "By all means, please do it. I'll remember this act of generosity and selflessness from you."

"Is it ever!" Richard said. "I'm not sure I'd make my most hated enemy do that. It's far more than just a sacrifice."

Ito held up both hands. "If there's one thing we must be careful of, it's taking pride in our humility. It just might counteract all the wonderful energy you've been sending to me."

Richard covered his mouth with both hands. "That's not what I meant at all."

Ito smiled. "It's okay. You're just exploring your path. But I wouldn't be much of a friend if I didn't point that out to you."

"Thank you," Richard said. "I'll try to keep that in mind for next time."

Richard spent the rest of the day keeping busy with other duties Ito had assigned along with praying in the temple. Growing up in Memphis, church was never optional. He appreciated the moral guidance he received there but hadn't considered Biblical teachings beyond that. The cultural importance of the Christian faith wasn't lost on him, and he saw that same type of devotion exhibited by the Buddhist monks. However, the practice of prayer was something he found mundane in every religious expression, save those moments when he was staring death in the face or his grief was too much to bear. And while he wasn't thrilled about the amount of time spent in the temple chanting prayers, Richard felt he needed some extra help if he was going to escape the mountain with pictures of the cipher.

After prayers, he sought out Bhodi near the front gate.

"Find what you were looking for?" Bhodi asked as soon as he noticed Richard.

"I thought this is a journey, not a treasure hunt," Richard said.

"Of course, but I—never mind."

Richard moved in close, continuing their conversation in hushed tones. "I'm being kicked out tomorrow morning and will be heading down the mountain. So, I'm going to need that ear."

"I'll have it for you before you leave," Bhodi said.

Richard nodded and patted Bhodi on the back. "You have a good evening."

After Richard returned to his room, he grabbed his camera and hid it beneath his robe. He proceeded to collect the supplies for cleaning the toilets and went to work. When he was finished, he ventured into the hidden room, keeping his head down to avoid drawing attention. Between quick glances, he was able to survey the room and get an idea of what was going on. Across the far side, several monks sat hunched over a desk, meticulously carving symbols into cylindrical pieces of wood. In the center of the room, a round table was stacked with finished ciphers. Men in suits inspected each one, examining every inch before putting down the device and moving to the next.

Richard meandered through the room until he reached the toilets in the back corner. No one seemed to pay him any attention. He needed to cause a diversion, to draw their attention away from the ciphers and enable him enough time to pocket one. But getting close wouldn't be easy given the number of men nearby. However, he noticed Saicho was talking with the outsiders.

That's my ticket to get close.

Richard approached the table, bucket in hand.

As he neared Saicho, the priest turned around when one of the men pointed at Richard.

"What are you doing in here, Mr. Halliburton?" Saicho asked. "Who gave you permission to enter this room?"

"I'm finishing up my final assignment to clean the toilets," Richard said.

"Are you sure? I swore I saw someone in here not ten

minutes ago cleaning them."

"That's what I was told to do," Richard said.

"By whom?"

"I don't know the monk's name," Richard said. "He saw me with a bucket and pointed me toward the door and made a cleaning motion."

"I'm sure you misunderstood. This area is restricted for craftsmen only."

"I see," Richard said as he palmed one of the ciphers and discreetly pulled it into his robe. "I won't complain about not having to clean latrines."

As Richard headed toward the exit, he saw Bhodi enter and cruise around the room. He never made eye contact with Richard, who was halfway out the door when he heard one of the men shout something in Japanese.

Richard didn't need a translator to know what they said: They'd just discovered a cipher was missing.

CHAPTER 18

RICHARD HUSTLED DOWN THE HALLWAY AND DUCKED down another corridor. He scanned the area to see if anyone had seen him, but it was clear. Without waiting another second, he dashed to the toilets, which were empty. He entered one of the stalls and pulled out his camera.

Setting up the cipher on a ledge, he started to take picture after picture, turning the device to capture all the different positions. He was almost finished when he heard footsteps just outside. As he scrambled to put away everything and hide the cipher, he was jolted in the back when the stall door swung open.

Richard swallowed hard as he rose to his feet. "That's no way to—"

He froze as he locked eyes with the man in front of him. It was Bhodi.

"What are you doing?" he asked.

"Would you believe me if I told you I was using the toilet?"

"Why was your back against the door? That's an odd position."

"I was just—"

Bhodi reached out and frisked Richard. He tried to step backward, but when he did, he bumped into the toilet and lost his grip on the cipher, which tumbled out from beneath his robe.

Bhodi knelt down to pick it up. "How do you explain this?"

"Well, I, uh—"

"You knew exactly what you were doing. You're a spy, aren't you? I should've known."

Richard placed his hands up in a posture of surrender. "I know this looks bad, but—"

"I don't want to hear your lame excuses. Do you realize the Kenpetai is involved with this project? They're going to kill you when I return this and tell them where I found it."

"Let's think this through," Richard said. "It doesn't have to happen like that. Don't forget that if I don't deliver proof of your death, the samurais are coming for you. And you'll suffer the same needless fate."

"Don't make this about me," Bhodi said.

Richard shrugged. "It is whether you want it to be or not. My fate is in your hands, so to speak. I'm dead if you turn me in. But you will be too. So, the real question is what do you want to do? Are you willing to sacrifice your life for a cipher that your country won't be using in a year from now anyway?"

Bhodi pursed his lips and eyed Richard carefully. "Damn you. I knew the priest should've denied you access to the monastery."

"What happens next is really simple," Richard said. "You sneak this back into the room and claim that you found it on the floor. Everyone will be relieved, you'll be a hero, and I'll be able to convince the blood-thirsty samurais down the mountain that you're dead."

"I don't like this."

"You don't have to like it," Richard said. "I'm not asking you to do anything immoral."

"You're asking me to lie."

"No, I'm asking you to pretend like you found the cipher on the floor. And refuse to tell anyone that we ever met and talked here."

"Fine," Bhodi said. "I'll go along with your little charade, but this is the last time I ever do anything for you."

"In that case, I promise not to ask anything else from you."

"Good," Bhodi said as he snatched the cipher from Richard and marched out of the bathroom toward the secret chamber.

Richard poked his head out of the room and peered in both directions to make sure no one noticed him. Satisfied that the corridor was empty, he eased into it and returned the cleaning supplies.

After he went back to his room, he rolled up his film and scrawled a word on there so he'd remember what it was: "Fuji Film". He stashed it in a pouch sewn into the wall of his backpack. When he picked it up to finish stuffing it, he found a small object wrapped in a piece of white cloth lying beneath the bag. He carefully peeled back the strips, revealing a severed ear. Richard gasped before covering it back up and tucking it away safely into his bag. Then he blew out his candle and went to bed. A few minutes went by and he didn't hear any shouting or yelling. And while he wasn't sure if Bhodi had succeeded, Richard felt like now was a good time to pray.

I need all the help I can get to escape this mountain with my life.

He fell to his knees at the foot of his bed and bowed his head, muttering a short but succinct prayer: "God, please help Bhodi. Amen."

* * *

BHODI TOOK A DEEP BREATH before tugging on the

handle to the secret room. Once he was ready to carry out the ruse, he headed toward the table where all the ciphers were being stacked. He gritted his teeth and knelt by the table, hesitating as he went to place the device on the ground.

The thought of betraying his country made him shudder. He'd fought in the war against Russia nearly twenty years earlier as an eighteen-year-old. While serving for Japan during that conflict, he met other soldiers who were still pining for the old ways of the samurai, which piqued his interest. And in a strange, meandering path, he found himself betraying his beloved country, the one he was willing to sacrifice his life for. He felt dirty. But being dirty was better than being dead, killed by the blade of his former samurai friends.

"Mite!" he shouted, holding up the device. "Did anyone notice this one beneath the table?" he asked in Japanese.

Prince Naruhiko picked it up and inspected it. Satisfied, he placed it back on the table and recounted the ciphers.

"They're all here," he announced, eliciting cheers from all the monks. The Kenpetai members' celebration was far more subdued.

Naruhiko shook Bhodi's hand, thanking him for what he'd done. Then the prince turned to Saicho, who was standing to the right. The entire conversation was within earshot of Bhodi, who strained to hear what they were saying as they talked softly.

"How did this happen?" Naruhiko asked.

Saicho shook his head. "I don't know. Someone must've lost count, and in the chaos one cipher got knocked off the top."

"I have half a mind to alter the cipher and start all over, but the general wants all these deployed as soon as possible so we can begin transmitting secret messages again among our intelligence operatives."

"I understand," Saicho said. "I will do my best to ensure this doesn't happen again."

"You better do more than that. Vow that it won't."

Saicho held up his right hand. "I swear it'll never happen again."

"Very good," Naruhiko said. "Now carry on."

Bhodi eased away from the two men, stealing toward the door. He put his hand on the doorknob and turned it before glancing over at Saicho, who was explaining to one of the craftsmen about a new procedure to make sure no cipher went missing for even a minute. Remaining frozen, Bhodi stared at Saicho. The priest caught the guard's eye.

"Did you need something?" Saicho asked.

Bhodi took a deep breath and exhaled. He swallowed hard before releasing the knob.

"Bhodi?" Saicho said again.

"Yes, as a matter of fact there is something I need to speak with you about. There's something you need to know."

CHAPTER 19

T HE NEXT MORNING, RICHARD AWOKE BEFORE MORNING prayers and checked his pack to make sure everything was in place. His camera, the film, the ear for the samurai warriors—everything was secured. As he pulled his pack over his shoulders, a knock at the door startled him.

Who could that be this early?

When Richard answered it, he found Saicho standing in the doorway, swinging a lantern in one hand while clutching a beaded necklace in the other. He eyed Richard cautiously.

"Did you think I was going to let you walk out of here without speaking to you first?" Saicho asked.

"I wanted to give myself plenty of time to get down the mountain in case I ran into any trouble."

Saicho stroked his chin. "Are you expecting trouble, my child?"

"Well, it's mountain climbing. You just never know what to expect. Better to proceed with caution."

"I see. Well, before you go, let's take a little walk."

Saicho gestured for Richard to exit his room. Despite the alarming visit and the odd behavior the priest exhibited, Richard steadied his breathing and nodded slowly.

"Of course," he said. "Is there something you wanted to talk about?"

Richard fell in lockstep with Saicho as they strolled along the corridor.

"I want to find out about your time here and get a sense for what you plan to write about the Shoshu Buddhists you met here and your general experience while at this monastery."

"To be honest, I learned a lot about myself. I'm not sure I'm anywhere close to enlightenment, but I feel like I have a better understanding of who I am."

"And who are you, Mr. Halliburton?" Saicho asked as he stopped and glared at Richard.

He was caught off guard by the sudden surge of animosity and stumbled backward until he bumped into the wall. His eyes widened as he tried to determine the true intent of Saicho's question.

"I'm a free spirit, an adventurer, a man who can't be bound by borders or inhibited by challenges."

"Like the challenge you're facing on your descent?"

Richard paused before nodding. "Yeah, it's not going to be easy. The storm that just blew through here isn't going to—"

"Enough," Saicho said with a growl as he moved within inches of Richard. "I saw the compassion you had for one of Mother Nature's broken and hurting creatures, and I broke one of my own rules: One moment doesn't define a person. While I have used that many times in extending grace to those who have made a mistake, I never considered the opposite side and how someone might be able to fool me by behaving a certain way for a short period of time."

"What are you trying to say?" Richard asked.

"I know who you are and what you are trying to do," Saicho said. "And while you may think it's noble, your deceit grieves me and has brought an unwelcome spirit into our sacred temple."

Richard slid to his left in an attempt to create some space between the two men. He was about to respond when he noticed Bhodi ease up behind Saicho.

"I'm sorry," Bhodi mouthed.

Richard glared at Bhodi. "How could you do this?"

"How could he do this?" Saicho asked before he poked Richard in the chest. "You are the one who shielded the truth about why you are here."

"I've never lied to you," Richard said.

Saicho scoffed. "Writing an article on Buddhism and Japan? You only sought refuge here when you were threatened with your life. And you thought you could just come in here and pretend like you were our friend when you had sinister plans all along."

"I'm not sure I understand," Richard said, holding to his story as long as possible.

"Give me your bag," Saicho said.

"What?" Richard said, tightening his grip on the straps.

"You heard me," Saicho said before glancing over his shoulder at Bhodi, who wrapped his hand around his dagger.

"Fine," Richard said. He handed his pack to Saicho.

The priest put the bag on the ground and knelt next to it, rifling through the contents.

"What are you searching for?" Richard asked. "I swear I didn't take anything from your temple here. I would never do that."

Richard craned his neck to see what Saicho was searching for. He grabbed every journal, flipping through the pages.

"What are you looking for?" Richard asked. "I didn't take anything."

After a few tense moments, Saicho pulled his hand out of the bag, holding up his fist triumphantly.

"This is what I was looking for," he declared.

Richard swallowed hard, hoping that what was in Saicho's hand wasn't what he feared.

"This," Saicho said, revealing a small object wrapped in cloth.

Richard sighed in relief, though it was only temporary.

Instead of being killed now, I'll be killed later.

"I'm sorry," Bhodi said. "I didn't want to get you in trouble, but I thought more about what I'd done, and I just could let a poor soul be desecrated in that way."

Richard closed his eyes and shook his head. "I was only trying to help."

Saicho stood. "And so was Bhodi, but then his conscience got the best of him and he realized how disrespectful this was to the deceased. Would you want someone dismembering you after your death?"

"I don't imagine I'll care very much then," Richard said with a shrug.

"Then you learned nothing while you were here. Before you go, I forbid you from ever writing about us, and I banish you from returning to any of our houses of worship. You have defiled this temple and enticed one of our fellow brothers to join you in a disgraceful act."

Richard placed his hands together in a gesture of prayer. "Please, I didn't know. I never meant to harm anyone. I was only trying to save Bhodi."

"Bhodi will have to atone for his own sins," Saicho said. "He doesn't need your help."

"Whatever you do, please don't blame him. It's my fault."

Saicho waved dismissively with the back of his hand at Richard. "We'll deal with Bhodi's punishment in whatever way we see fit. But I urge you to leave now before word of this reaches members of the council."

"Of course," Richard said as he bowed his head.

Richard flung his pack over his shoulder and hustled down the hallway and through the gates. Saicho shuffled behind him, ushering him outside.

The sun peeked over the horizon in the distance, illuminating the eastern side of Mt. Fuji. A cold wind nipped at Richard's extremities, stealing whatever bit of warmth he'd had inside the mountain.

Both men stopped and took in the scene.

"Glorious view, isn't it?" Saicho said.

Richard eyed him cautiously. "Sure is."

"Enjoy it because it'll be the last time you see it. If I ever see you around here again, we'll deal far more harshly with you."

Lines creased Richard's forehead. "I thought you were all about peace."

"We are," Saicho sneered. "And we're all about keeping it too. Now I suggest you run along so you have enough time to make the descent today. It looks like another storm is headed this way."

Richard returned to the path that led him to the monastery. However, he stopped and looked back to see that Saicho was gone.

Finally alone, Richard sat on a rock and contemplated his next steps. While he wanted to go down the familiar route, he considered his immediate future, which was sure to include a clash with the samurais. That wasn't his preference. Without proof of Bhodi's death, Richard needed to plot a different way off the mountain, anything to avoid dying at the hands of vengeful warriors.

He ventured around the edge of the mountain and peered at the route along the eastern side. That route was supposedly far more difficult to climb up or down. But he didn't care.

Richard cinched his straps, pulling them tight on his shoulders before he stopped and glanced upward.

If I hurry, I can make it to the top.

Richard checked his watch. At two minutes before 7:00 a.m., he figured he'd have just enough time to reach the summit before heading back down, and going in a route that would avoid the samurais.

Richard put on his boots and began the climb. Despite windier conditions closer to the top, he soldiered on. After two hours, he proclaimed victory as he reached the summit. He raised his hands to celebrate and was knocked over by a strong gust. He managed to regain his footing and proceeded to pack for the journey home after grabbing a quick picture from the top.

The return trip was more treacherous than the ascent. After the storm, the ice had hardened overnight, making digging his spikes into the thick surface more challenging than ever. And small slips became harrowing, as he sometimes slid ten or fifteen feet down the mountain before managing to get a foothold.

After four hours, he stopped to take a break. His legs ached from the pressure he put them under while heading downward. While it was almost 3:00 p.m., Richard could tell from how low the sun hung in the sky that he didn't have much time. He drank some water before resuming his descent.

At 4:30 p.m., he considered that he had at least an hour or more remaining. He also figured that most of that would need to be done in the dark, a none-too exciting prospect.

He came to a small plateau and sat down for another short break. With his toes already numb, Richard now couldn't feel his face. Spending the night on the side of Mt. Fuji would surely prove disastrous, if not fatal. That thought spurred him to leap to his feet and continue along.

However, the creaking of ice made him stop and turn around to find the source. When he did, he saw the samurai warriors fanning out to form a semicircle around him. As Richard walked backward in an effort to stay away from them, they closed in around him. After a few more steps, he realized that there wasn't anywhere else for him to go. He peered behind him, glancing over his shoulder at the landscape that seemed to disappear into the burgeoning night.

"Mr. Halliburton," Hattori Mitsunari said, his weapon drawn, the tip pointed at Richard, "did you think we wouldn't find you?"

Richard stopped and glared at Mitsunari. "I will not be held captive by you."

Mitsunari threw his head back and laughed, joined by all the men who were with him after translating Richard's statement.

"Did you think I didn't meant what I said earlier?" Mitsunari asked. "When I said if you didn't bring us proof that you murdered Bhodi, we would make sure you took his place? So, where's the evidence?"

Richard held up his right hand and then sank to the ground. "Just a minute, I have it for you, but I have to retrieve it in my bag.

Richard sifted through his backpack. He caught Mitsunari staring out across the horizon before glancing back at Richard digging through his things.

"I know it's in here somewhere," Richard said. "Just give me a minute."

The longer Richard's exercise in stalling went, the more restless Mitsunari became. "Mr. Halliburton, we're running out of daylight. And you're running out of time. Now show me something before I have to assume that you're lying."

"What I'm looking for is in here," Richard said. "I just know it."

"What are you doing?" Mitsunari asked. "Do you intend to fight all of us? I can promise you that such an effort will not end well."

Before Mitsunari could say another word, a wry smiled spread across Richard's face.

Then he took off running away from the other soldiers. As he neared the edge, he took a flying leap into the dusky sky.

CHAPTER 20

RICHARD CLOSED HIS EYES AND TRIED TO REMEMBER everything Thomas Orde-Lees had explained about how to operate a parachute while jumping off a stationary object. Don't wait too long before deploying your chute.

The wind seared Richard's face as he dove toward the bottom. Tears welled in his eyes as he zoomed toward the earth. Richard counted in his head before tugging hard on the string.

In an instant, the blast of air that had been assaulting his face stopped, providing him with a much-needed respite. His body jerked upward before continuing a new trajectory that included a much slower descent. The wind swung him around, giving him a view of the mountain. Looking halfway up, he saw the samurais standing on the ledge of the plateau and shaking their weapons.

Richard smiled and gave them a taunting wave. For the first time in days, he wasn't worried about maintaining his cover in a monastery full of monks working for the enemy or fulfilling his assignment to sword-wielding warriors. Instead, he basked in the grandeur of the moment, drinking in the last few minutes of twilight before darkness enveloped the land.

He hit the ground hard but remembered Lees's instruction to immediately roll in order to absorb the impact.

Despite the jarring landing, Richard hopped to his feet, feeling fine as ever. Working quickly, he gathered up the parachute and stuffed it into his pack.

While he was scrambling to wad up his chute, he didn't notice the small group of people who stared at him in awe. A man stood outside a bus and shouted at the crowd, motioning for them to come to him. Slowly, each man and woman peeled their eyes away from Richard and trudged toward the bus. Upon not seeing any other transportation options, he followed after them.

"Can I get a ride back to Tokyo?" Richard asked. "I can pay."

The driver didn't understand and scowled as he studied Richard up and down. After waving him off, the driver turned to leave. Richard, fearing that he might get stranded, grabbed the man's arm with one hand. In the other, Richard jangled a purse full of yens. That was a sound the man understood. He quickly held out his hand before relenting and inviting Richard to board.

Richard navigated his way through the crowded bus before taking the last remaining seat on the end, three rows from the back. He sat in silence as he felt the entire bus full of people staring at him, shooting fire at him. The bus sputtered as the driver wheeled it around the parking lot and navigated to the main road. They traveled several miles before anyone spoke. But when they finally did, he was pleasantly surprised.

"What is that contraption?" the man asked.

Richard looked at the man and smiled. "It's called a parachute. Have you ever seen one of these before?"

The man shook his head. "Not in person. I've read about them and seen pictures of them, but never witnessed one in use."

His grasp of the English language put Richard at ease. "Where did you learn to speak such fluent English?"

"I know I may look like most Japanese, but my mother was an American," he said.

Richard cocked his head to one side. "Fascinating. How did your parents meet?"

"They met in San Francisco while he was in port after serving on a shipping vessel. She was the cook at their boarder house. They fell in love, and she moved back to Tokyo with him. And, as they say, the rest is history."

Richard shook his head. "It's an amazing world we live in, isn't it?"

The man nodded in agreement. "What were you doing up there this afternoon?"

"I hiked to the summit of Mt. Fuji," Richard said.

The man chuckled. "You're quite a rascal with that tale."

Richard shrugged. "Believe me or not, but earlier today I was at the top. If I could show you these pictures, I would. But I have to get them developed."

"It's far too dangerous to reach the top of Mt. Fuji in the winter. No one has ever made done that."

"Until today," Richard said, flashing a wide grin. "Of course, that was only half as challenging as escaping a band of samurai warriors."

The man shifted in his seat. "Did you fight your way out?"

"That's what the parachute was for."

"You're a smart man. They would've carved you up."

Richard nodded. "Especially since I didn't have anything to fight them with."

"If you try to play their game, you will regret it. But if you can take another escape route, you'll have a chance."

"Sounds like you have some personal experience with them."

"Once," the man said. "A long time ago."

"And how did you avoid getting killed?"

"The legend of suzumebachi."

"Suzumebachi?" Richard asked, his eye widening. "Who's that?"

Several people sitting nearby started chuckling, making Richard wonder if more people knew English than he suspected. He scanned the smiling faces and then cracked a faint smile.

"What? Was it something I said?"

"Suzumebachi isn't a person. It's an insect. In America, you call it a hornet. But here, we call it a suzumebachi with one major difference."

"And what's that?" Richard asked.

"It's poisonous and quite lethal."

Richard, seeing an opportunity to include this story in his article, pulled out his journal and started taking notes. "So, there's a legend around this bug?"

"In a manner of speaking, yes. The ancient samurais revered the suzumebachi. At some point, warriors began using them as a test to determine if their enemies were lying. If someone survived a suzumebachi bite, they were seen as someone who was to be trusted and freed. The process became known as the 'Suzumebachi Test'. If you were captured and demanded to be given the test and survived it, you were set free."

"Sounds like it's somewhat similar to the pirate version of parlay," Richard said.

The man nodded. "However, there is some danger involved since they aren't required to release you. But more often than not, they do since the insect usually doesn't inject a person with enough poison to kill them."

"How does the poison kill?"

"I've never seen it happen, but I've heard that your breathing passageways are blocked and you suffocate to death, as if someone is choking you."

Richard shuddered. "Sounds awful."

"That's why the suzumebachi are both feared and revered. Many Buddhist traditions discourage killing any insects, so they thrive and kill people here every year."

"Thank you for the lesson," Richard said as he tucked his journal back into his bag.

"Yes, so next time you run into samurais and don't have a parachute, you can demand to be put to the Suzumebachi Test."

"I'm not sure that sounds like a great direction to go."

"Better than sure death," the man said. He leaned over and spoke in a hushed tone. "And they're not nearly as lethal as everyone makes them out to be. But don't say that too loud or people will get upset."

Richard nodded knowingly before settling in for the rest of the ride back to Tokyo.

When the bus finally came to a stop near the city center, Richard threw his pack over his shoulder and then hustled down the steps. He recognized the location, which was only a few blocks from his hotel.

As he rounded the corner leading to his hotel, someone tugged on Richard's collar, pulling him backward.

"Hey!" Richard exclaimed as he was released. He stumbled in an attempt to regain his balance before finally reaching an upright position. "What's the meaning of—" Richard said before he froze, recognizing the man in front of him. "Oh, it's you."

Thomas Orde-Lees gave Richard a shove in the chest, pushing him back into the alley. However, the former British soldier didn't say a word.

"What's the meaning of this?" Richard demanded.

Lees put his index finger to his lips.

"What is it?" Richard asked in a whisper.

Lees peered onto the street, looking in both directions before ducking back into the alley.

"Will you please tell me what's going on?" Richard asked.

"You can't go back to your hotel," Lees said.

"Why not?"

"The Kenpetai is looking for you. They know you're a spy."

CHAPTER 21

RICHARD RUBBED HIS FACE AND CONSIDERED THE implications. His time in Japan was coming to an abrupt end, while his greatest fear was being realized. Despite his deep patriotism, he didn't want to die in a Japanese prison somewhere. He always envisioned himself dying on a grand adventure. But caged up only to be shot or hung was not the blaze of glory he preferred when his life had run its course.

Lees shook Richard. "Hey, man. Are you still with me? Did you hear what I just said?"

Richard nodded. "I heard you. I'm just trying to think about what this means."

"It means they're going to kill you once they catch you, which you can't let happen, especially now."

"Why now?"

"Did you get the cipher?"

Richard nodded. "Well, I got pictures of it."

"That's massive. Between our governments' cryptology departments, they should be able to use those images to piece together how the device works and start decrypting messages right away."

"I still have to get out of here."

"Don't worry," Lees said. "I've got you covered there."

"What do I need to do?"

Lees crammed a change purse into Richard's hands. "There's enough money in here for you to catch the next train in half an hour to the coast."

"The coast?"

"Yes, Chosi," Lees explained. "You can leave from the port there on a ship heading straight for Seattle first thing in the morning."

"I need to confirm this with my contacts here at the consulate," Richard said.

"You can't. The Kenpetai will capture you before you get inside and arrest you."

"This isn't exactly protocol," Richard said.

"You're going to worry about protocol in a situation like this? If you don't listen to me, everything here will have been for naught and you can kiss your precious writing career goodbye along with the rest of your life. If I were you, this wouldn't be the moment I'd pick to be pigheaded about something."

"I apologize if my response comes across as defiant, but Hank Foster told me to be wary of trusting anyone, advice well worth heeding in my experience."

Lees took a deep breath and exhaled slowly. "Did you use my parachute?"

Richard removed his pack and handed the parachute to Lees.

"I'm taking that as a yes," Lees said as he stuffed the parachute into his own pack.

Richard nodded subtly.

"So, if I wanted the cipher for myself, I would've sabotaged this," Lees said. "I swear you can trust me. And I've got a secret entrance for you along with a way to get into your room without getting caught."

Lees handed Richard a rope.

"What's this for?" he asked.

"It'll help you descend to your room."

"I've done enough of that for today."

Lees eyed Richard closely. "Did you summit Mt. Fuji?"

Richard closed his eyes and nodded as he started to seethe upon learning that he wouldn't be falling into a comfortable bed and getting a good night of sleep.

"You can get into your room on the third floor, grab your stuff, and then get out of there," Lees said.

"I've got a better idea. Why don't you do it for me?"

"I would," Lees said before pointing to his arm. "I had a little mishap yesterday. I dislocated my shoulder. Climbing is not an option for me."

"Fine," Richard said with a growl before snatching the rope. "Just tell me what to do."

Lees explained the route Richard needed to take in order to avoid detection. Once he reached the balcony of his new room located just above his old one on the fourth floor, Richard could tie off the rope, repel down, grab his belongings, and climb back up.

"You think this will work?"

Lees nodded.

"And if it doesn't?"

Lees shrugged. "You can always head straight to the train station if you want to leave everything here."

"No," Richard snapped. "I haven't traveled all over the world for the past couple of years to just abandon all my notes and journals in my room."

"That's what I thought. Now get going before it gets too late. The train leaves in an hour."

Richard followed the directions, shimmying down the rope into his room. He quietly slipped inside and gathered the clothes and journals he'd left behind for his trip to

Taiseki-ji's hidden monastery. As he was stuffing everything inside his bag, he noticed an envelope addressed to him sitting on the foot of the bed.

Richard opened the correspondence, pulling out a dance card with his name on it. He smiled as he read the note from Hisako.

> Dearest Richard,
>
> Thank you for everything you've done for me the past few days. I learned that my intuition about Prince Naruhiko was wrong. He didn't want to kill me; he wanted to reward me. Someone lied to me. However, if they hadn't, I would've likely killed you, like I did the man on the train.
>
> I have much to figure out, as I'm sure you do too. Thank you for all the wonderful memories, and I wish you the best in your future endeavors.
>
> All the best,
>
> H
>
> P.S. I can't wait to read your book.

Richard tucked the letter into his back pocket before making one final sweep of the room. When he was satisfied that he had everything, he returned to the balcony. But as Richard began his ascent up one floor, he heard someone shouting from above. Richard looked up and saw two members of Kenpetai pointing at him.

Richard muttered a few choice words beneath his breath and decided to deviate from the original plan. He stepped over the balcony railing and crouched low as he clung to the bars. Lowering himself so his feet were dangling over the second floor balcony, he swung back and forth until he had enough momentum to land there.

The Kenpetai officers overhead continued shouting and were now blowing their whistles. Richard looked up at them and waved before he leaped over the balcony and landed on the sidewalk, rolling for a few feet before springing up onto his feet. Then he broke into a dead sprint, darting down the alleyway where he'd met Lees.

"What are you doing?" Lees asked. "I heard all that commotion and guessed someone had spotted you."

"I don't have time to explain," Richard said as he dug into his pack and grabbed a small pouch of used film canisters, his camera, and his journals. "Give me your bag."

"It's a wadded up parachute."

"I don't care. Give it to me now."

"All right," Lees said as he handed it over.

"And your jacket too," Richard said, snapping his fingers. "Okay, okay."

Lees removed his coat and exchanged it with Richard. Moments later, he was strolling down the street toward the train station in the opposite direction of Lees, who was running for his life.

Richard smiled when he glanced over his shoulder and saw Lees disappear into a nearby wooded park. Then Richard picked up his pace and arrived at the station just in time before the 10:15 p.m. train for Chosi. The trip took three hours, putting Richard in the port city with more than enough time to purchase a ticket and board the steamship President Madison for the week-long trip to Seattle.

As Richard sat on the platform at the train station, he kept his head low in an effort not to draw any attention to himself. He felt relaxed, satisfied that he'd accomplished his mission.

At 10:00 a.m., the conductor called for boarding as passengers shuffled near their train. One by one, the people forked over their passes and climbed up the steps. Once the last ticket had been collected, he made one final announcement. After a brief delay, the train started to chug out of the station.

Richard sighed in relief, all alone in his compartment. He leaned back in his seat, resting his head and closing his eyes. However, his peaceful moment was interrupted by a man shouting outside and running along the platform. Richard leaned near the window to see what the commotion was about.

He recognized the man shouting. It was Yutaka.

Richard did a double take to confirm his suspicion. And there was little doubt that the pudgy Kenpetai officer outside was the same man who'd been assigned with following Richard.

Richard went to check a final time only to watch Yutaka pull himself aboard.

CHAPTER 22

RICHARD CLENCHED HIS FISTS IN PREPARATION FOR A fight. He opened his compartment just wide enough to poke his head out and peer down the aisle. His notion that he'd brawl with Yutaka ended the moment Richard noticed the gun in the officer's hand.

Yutaka glared at Richard once the two men made eye contact. "Did you think you could run from me forever?"

"I'm sure you can appreciate the fact that I'm not the kind of person who likes being followed day and night," Richard said, raising his hands in the air. "I only came to Tokyo to deliver some mail to the embassy."

Yutaka shook his head. "Perhaps that's what you came for, but that's not all you did while you were here."

"I did make a short trip to Mt. Fuji, and now I'm headed home," Richard said. "There's really not that much more to tell."

"Where's your bag?" Yutaka asked.

"It's in my compartment. I have no idea what you're looking for, but you're more than welcome to go through my things if you don't believe me."

Yutaka used his gun to gesture for Richard to go. Once they reached the compartment, Richard grabbed his pack and pulled it open for Yutaka.

"Here," Richard said, dropping it on the floor. "See for yourself."

He watched Yutaka closely as the Kenpetai officer sifted through all the contents. Several times, Yutaka stopped and held up an object, examining it. When he reached a stack of journals, he held them up before scanning the pages.

"It's just my record of my visits and my adventures. I don't know what you're looking for, but you're not going to find anything other than that."

"Ah, ha!" Yutaka exclaimed as he leaped to his feet. "This is it. Listen to this passage."

Yutaka read a passage from Richard's journal about his trip to China where Japanese soldiers escaped from an ancient chamber with a large cache of treasures.

"I don't know what that proves," Richard said. "That I was on an archeological dig when I ran across some Japanese soldiers. It happens all the time whenever I'm traveling. I happen to meet military from other countries."

"And what about this?" Yutaka asked as he held up Richard's pouch of used film.

Richard kept his composure as Yutaka inspected each canister. "Those are from all the pictures I took during my world trip and what I intend to use in my book."

"You're writing a book?"

"That's my dream—and it's the whole reason I came to Japan. I've been fascinated with Mt. Fuji for a long time. I wanted to see it for myself and climb it."

"And did you?" Yutaka asked.

"That's my proof right there," Richard said, nodding at the roll in Yutaka's hand.

"'Fuji film'," Yutaka read aloud. "Hmmm."

"Yes, that's the roll with all my pictures of my summit of Mt. Fuji."

Yutaka raised an eyebrow as he studied Richard. "You climbed Mt. Fuji while you were here?"

"Yes, earlier today," Richard said. "If you don't believe me, you'll have to buy my book."

Yutaka thrust the pack into Richard's hands. "Unfortunately for you, it's not my job to determine if you are a spy and in our country illegally. I was tasked with following you during your stay here, something I failed to do. But I won't fail this time. We'll be getting off at the next stop, and I will take you to Kenpetai headquarters."

"I'm sorry, but that's not going to work for me," Richard said. "I have to be on a ship first thing in the morning to return home to see my mother. She's deathly ill. If you delay me in any way, it's possible that I won't be able to see her before she passes."

"I don't believe you," Yutaka said.

"I have a letter from her right here in my bag," Richard said. "I'll show it to you."

He fell to his knees on the floor and rummaged through his backpack. Yutaka kept his gun trained on Richard. After a few tense seconds, Richard shook his head and sighed.

"I know it was in here," he said. "You didn't take it, did you?"

Yutaka scowled. "Get ready because we're about to get off at the next station."

Richard slumped his shoulders and hung his head as he stared down into his bag. Yet Yutaka didn't appear to be buying the ruse. So, Richard took a deep breath before exploding to his feet and swinging his bag, knocking Yutaka's gun out of his hand.

Richard tossed his pack aside while Yutaka went for the weapon on the ground. But Richard stomped on Yutaka's hand, drawing a yelp from the portly investigator. Then with a knee to the face, Yutaka's head snapped backward, slamming hard against the wall and knocking him out.

The lights along the track flickered, signaling that the next station was fast approaching. Richard pocketed the gun and then opened the door to his compartment to check for any witnesses. Satisfied that the corridor was empty, he lugged Yutaka to the bathroom, tying his hands together with a belt and gagging his mouth with a spare shirt.

For almost the entire ride, Richard remained with Yutaka, knocking him out time and time again whenever regained consciousness. However, Richard recognized he desperately needed to push Yutaka out of the train prior to reaching Chosi.

Richard returned to his seat for a few minutes as he heard the conductor walking through the car to check on all the passengers. He said something in Japanese to Richard, who smiled and nodded. After the man left, Richard hustled back to the bathroom to check on Yutaka. But Yutaka was gone.

Richard cursed under his breath as he looked up and down the hallway for the investigator. There wasn't any sign of him.

That's when Richard heard the door at the opposite end bang as it closed. He raced toward the noise and found Yutaka between cars. Richard pulled out the weapon, training it on the escapee.

"That's far enough," Richard said as he stepped outside. The wind whipped past, and the wheels were clicking along the track.

Yutaka stopped and looked over his shoulder at Richard. "Has your mother made a miraculous recovery?"

Richard clenched his jaw, steadying the gun with both hands.

"Stop pretending like you're going to shoot me," Yutaka

said. "You don't have it in you."

The train slowed as it made a wide turn and eased onto a bridge. Richard glanced down at the water. He decided he didn't need a gun.

Richard grabbed the handrails, giving him the leverage he needed to swing back and unleash a furious kick at Yutaka's head. The inspector wobbled before his head smashed into the side of the car. With one swift push, Richard used his feet to propel the unconscious Yutaka into the Tone River below.

Richard peered into the water to confirm Yutaka had made it. His body sank before quickly resurfacing. He was facedown, bobbing with the rhythm of the tide encroaching from the Pacific Ocean.

A half-hour later, the train pulled into Chosi a few minutes before 1:00 a.m. Richard grabbed his bag before exiting and hustling through the station. He found the main road and followed Lees's instructions on how to find the dock where the President Madison was leaving from. After a brief search, he located the steamship and picked out a nearby spot to catch a few hours of sleep before boarding for the 7:00 a.m. departure.

* * *

RICHARD AWOKE to the sun peeking over the horizon and the bustling of the dock workers rushing to load all the last-minute supplies for the long trip. He prepared to board but was told that the President Madison needed to undergo some last-minute repairs, delaying the voyage. The captain said that he would blow the horn when they had another announcement regarding when the ship would be ready.

Richard returned to his spot to catch a few more hours of sleep. He quickly drifted off and didn't awake again until he felt someone kicking at his legs.

Squinting at the daylight suddenly flooding his vision, Richard put his hand up to his forehead to shield his eyes. The moment he recognized the man kneeling down a few feet, Richard bolted to his feet, grabbed his pack, and took off running. However, he didn't get more than twenty yards before he was tackled from behind.

Hattori Mitsunari laughed as he eyed Richard, who was pinned to the ground by two other samurais. "You didn't think we were just going to let you get away without sufficient payment for passage, did you?"

Richard barely recognized Mitsunari, who wasn't wearing his traditional warrior garb. Instead, he donned a suit, complete with a dark tie and a pair of sunglasses. However, he still had his sword, which he was resting on.

"How did you . . ." Richard paused, struggling to escape the grasp of the men.

"It wasn't too difficult to find out where the flying man went," Mitsunari said. "You made quite an impression. And unfortunately for you, that's why we're here. You better just be glad we found you first, since we'll make this quick. If the Kenpetai had caught you, you would be spending a significant part of your life in prison."

"If you're wanting me to thank you, you'll be waiting a long time," Richard said with a sneer.

"I don't care as long as you suffer," Mitsunari said before nodding at his fellow warriors. "Bring him with me."

They yanked Richard to his feet and nudged him toward a nearby alley and out of plain sight.

"Is this really necessary?" Richard asked. "Can't we let bygones be bygones?"

"No," Mitsunari said. "You accepted the deal were offered, and you didn't fulfill your half. Now you must suffer the penalty for your transgression."

"Transgression sounds so harsh, don't you think?"

Mitsunari directed two men to force Richard to his knees and pull on his arms, creating a clean path for the blade to come down and remove his head from his body.

"Have any last words?" Mitsunari asked as he drew his sword back.

"As a matter of fact, I do," Richard said. "I'd like to be given the Suzumebachi Test."

Mitsunari sighed and shook his head. "Who told you about that? That's an ancient practice."

"Like being a samurai?" Richard asked.

One of the men walked up to Mitsunari and whispered in his ear. Then the leader turned back toward Richard.

"You know, on second thought, we're going to give it to you," Mitsunari said. "We happen to have a suzumebachi with us. Plus, my fellow warrior reminded me that it'd be a lot easier to explain than a severed head discovered in a back alley. So, you're coming with me. We're going to do this in public."

Mitsunari snatched a nearby crate and pulled it into the middle of the street running in front of the docks. Plenty of anxious travelers with nothing to do were arrested by Mitsunari's call to watch the spectacle. He waited for a couple minutes until a crowd of about fifty people had gathered around.

"Ladies and gentlemen, I realize many of you may be about to depart from our beloved country," Mitsunari began. "However, before you go, you're going to witness a treat: the Suzumebachi Test. Now, you're probably asking yourself, 'What is the Suzumebachi Test?' and that's a good question. The truth is this used to be an ancient practice in Japan."

He held up a small container with a suzumebachi inside.

"You might know these insects as hornets where you

come from, but here they are known as suzumebachi—and they can kill you. Now, our good friend here, Mr. Halliburton, broke his word to me and has opted for the Suzumebachi Test instead of suffering the consequences. The good thing is this little bug will tell us if he was lying or not based on his survival. Are you ready?"

The crowd cheered, something Richard found disturbing, though not surprising. Traveling vaudeville shows were still popular and contained magicians in their entertainment lineup. He figured most of the people present didn't realize this was not a trick.

Mitsunari explained how the test worked. When he finished, he whipped the crowd up into an excited frenzy.

"Are you ready to see if this man deserves to die?" he asked.

Affirmed by cheers and shouts and clapping, Mitsunari nodded knowingly at two of his men, who grabbed Richard's right arm. They pushed back his sleeve as Mitsunari loosed the lid to the small glass jar. When he was ready, he pulled the top off and quickly flipped over the container, pressing it against Richard's arm.

The crowd gasped as the suzumebachi darted back and forth in the jar, confused by all the activity. Then it settled onto Richard's arm and injected a dose of poison into it. Richard gritted his teeth, writhing back and forth for a few seconds.

He suddenly felt very drowsy, fighting to keep his eyes open. After a brief moment, everything faded to black.

CHAPTER 23

RICHARD BLINKED A FEW TIMES AS HE REGAINED consciousness. Part of the crowd was still gathered around him, curious as to whether he would survive or not. When he sat up, the people applauded. Richard staggered to his feet and scanned the faces for Mitsunari.

"Where was the man who did this to me?" Richard asked.

"The Japanese man and the rest of his street act went that way," one woman said, pointing south down the road.

Richard rushed over to check his bag. He muttered a few curse words under his breath before he stumbled to the ground.

He remained out for a few minutes but came to when he heard a familiar voice.

"Richard," the woman said. "Richard, can you hear me?"

He opened his eyes to see Hisako standing over him, lines creasing her forehead.

"What happened?" she asked.

"He was stung by a wasp," one of the men nearby said.

The elderly woman next to him hit the man in the arm with her purse and shook her head. "No, William, it was a hornet. Weren't you paying attention?"

Hisako stood and eyed the woman closely. "Did the man who did this say anything about it being a suzumebachi?"

The old woman nodded. "Yeah, suzu-something. I don't know. Sounds like what you said. I can't say that word."

"That's what I needed to know," Hisako said. "Thank you."

She helped Richard to his feet and asked someone to get him a drink of water.

"Am I going to be okay?" Richard asked.

"You'll be just fine. You just need to get some water you in to flush out what's left of that poison."

Richard took a deep breath and exhaled slowly. The audience that had crowded around him dispersed, rushing rapidly to the docks when the fog horn sounded.

"What are you doing here?" Richard asked. "I got your note, but I didn't think I'd ever see you again."

"Somebody dragged me down here just to keep an eye on you and make sure you got on board the President Madison," she said.

"And who was that?" Richard asked.

"Me," Lees said as he strode up to them, lugging Richard's backpack over one shoulder.

Richard flashed a quick smile before remembering he hadn't seen the bag Lees had given him.

"Where'd it go?" Richard asked.

"Are you looking for this?" Hisako asked as she held out his bag.

"Yes," he said before grabbing it and rifling through the contents. When he finished, he started seething.

"What is it?" she asked.

"My camera," Richard said. "The samurais took my camera."

"You mean this one?" Lees asked, dangling a camera in front of Richard's face.

"How did you—"

"When I got here, those men were running away. I chased them down and got your bag back. I let them go with just the cash purse."

"You what?" Richard asked.

"It's just money," Lees said, tossing another pouch at Richard.

"Thank you," he said. "I don't care about the money, but that camera is like gold to me."

The foghorn sounded again as people hustled up the ramp to get on the steamship.

"Looks like they're going to leave you if you don't hustle," Lees said.

Richard nodded and smiled. "So, is this a real goodbye this time or are we just pretending again?"

"I guess you'll find out soon enough," Lees said.

Richard hugged Hisako and Lees then stepped back a few feet. "You two make a great couple. Good luck."

Hisako blushed. "Good luck to you, Richard. You're going to need it more than we will."

Lees saluted Richard before turning and racing toward the ramp.

Richard showed his pass to the ticket taker at the edge of the dock and then hustled aboard. He glanced over his shoulder and waved at his companions one final time. But he was so excited to finally be returning home that he didn't notice the portly Kenpetai inspector walking up the ramp thirty yards behind him.

CHAPTER 24

AFTER RESTING FOR THE FIRST TWENTY-FOUR HOURS at sea, Richard decided to explore the ship and see if there were any social gatherings that evening. He relished the opportunity to meet other travelers and expand his network. As he cruised from deck to deck, he didn't find the type of gatherings that piqued his interest: a political discussion, a poetry reading group, and a seminar instructing people how to knit. Then he came to the ballroom dance floor.

"Couples' dance tonight at 7 p.m.," he read as he looked at the sign.

Now that's my kind of gathering.

He retreated to his room to buff his shoes and try to get his shirt and jacket out with the least amount of wrinkles. Despite his efforts to keep everything neat and tidy, he'd experienced so many adventures over the past couple of years that having anything suitable for a formal setting was nothing more than a dream. He sifted through his bag and found one shirt that only had a grease stain just below his elbow. Seeing the oxford button-down as his only real option, he put it on and rolled up his sleeves, obscuring the mark from view.

Until the event began, he meandered around the ship, greeting others passengers and making small talk with them. He met two bankers and a college president, along with two young women who were returning to the U.S. after touring Japan as part of a vaudeville show.

One of the women, Mabel, told Richard that she swallowed fire as part of her act. He was fascinated with her tales of rural Japan as well as how she readied herself to eat fire.

"It's really quite simple," she explained. "Just a little bit of mind over matter. That's how it is with all pain. If you can focus on something else rather than the burning sensation for just a moment or two, that's all you need for your mouth to extinguish the flame."

"That's all you do?" Richard asked.

She winked and patted him on his hand. "All I'm going to tell you. Remember, a good magician never reveals his secrets."

Richard shook his head as his mouth hung agape. "Swallowing fire? Incredible."

"I also cut a mean rug," she said before breaking into a few dance moves and shimmying across the floor. "Do you dance?"

Richard smiled wryly. "I don't consider what I do dancing."

"Two left feet, huh?"

"More like I become one with the music—and my partner, of course."

She smiled. "I look forward to getting you on my dance card tonight."

"Likewise," Richard said before kissing the woman on the hand.

He waved goodbye before spinning and heading along the deck, continuing his search for other gatherings where he could meet people he related to. He wandered to the dining room and grabbed a bite to eat before going to his room for a short nap.

When he awoke, he got dressed and danced in front of the mirror for a half-hour to make sure he hadn't forgotten all his moves. He hadn't. After dinner, he helped the staff clear the chairs and tables, pushing them along the wall and opening a sizable spot in the center of the room. In one corner, a string quartet took its position and began tuning all its instruments.

"This isn't like most formal dances," one of the staff members said as he helped Richard line more furniture along the wall.

"What do you mean?" he asked.

"It's going to be the best you've ever witnessed—at least on a steamship."

"Then let's get this party started."

Fifteen minutes later, the ship's orchestra took the stage and played a few songs to get warmed up. Richard managed to secure a slot for all twelve of the songs on the dance cards. Mabel penciled him in for both a fox trot and a waltz, angling for even more before he suggested that wouldn't be very polite.

During their first dance, Richard focused on his moves, putting on a show. Halfway through the song, the conductor grabbed the microphone and said he was going to speed things up, challenging partners to do the same. As the cadence increased, Richard stayed on beat and helped Mabel keep time. By the end, they were the only two on the floor, as a delighted audience looked on.

But in the second dance, Richard didn't feel the need to impress Mabel with his skills and instead engaged her in a conversation.

"Do you think you can just make women melt because of your dancing prowess?" she asked.

"Who said that's what I'm doing?" Richard asked.

"Maybe I simply like dancing."

"From my experience, men hate dancing. They only learn how to do it so they can impress women."

"I'm not like all men."

Mabel leaned in a little closer. "No, you're not."

Richard switched directions as he flashed a smile.

When they came back together, she eyed him closely. "Do you realize there's a man in the corner who's been watching you all night?"

"I wasn't aware," Richard said. "When I start dancing, I only focus on one thing."

"You sure you can't focus on two things?" she asked with a wink.

Richard shook his head. "It's a curse, I guess."

"Well, that guy over there has been watching you like a hawk all night," she said. "It's getting a little creepy. It's like he wants to get on your dance card."

"Good thing I don't have one."

She chuckled. "The way he's been staring at you, I think he might just walk up and ask you, dance card or not."

"Describe him."

"He's short, Japanese, tightly cropped dark hair, and smoking a cigar."

"Not sure he's the kind of dance partner I'm looking for."

She chuckled. "You're obviously exactly what he's looking for as he hasn't taken his eyes off you since you walked in the room."

Richard discreetly peeked where Mabel was looking as he whirled her around. Once he placed his back to the man, Richard locked eyes with her.

"When this song ends, I want you to help me vanish," he said.

"Is there something wrong?"

Richard nodded. "Just stay calm, but that man is trying to either kill me or arrest me. And if I had to pick, my money would be on the former."

Mabel's eyes widened. "You know him?"

"Unfortunately, yes. Though he's the last person I expected to see on this voyage."

"So you have a stalker?"

"A hunter," he corrected. "Now come with me so I can disappear in the crowd."

Once the song ended, Richard took Mabel's hand and charged straight into the throng of people standing around waiting for the next dance. The couple ducked out through a side door and into the hallway.

"You're starting to scare me," she said.

"Look, if you know what's best for you, go back inside and dance with your next partner," Richard said. "You don't deserve to get caught up in the middle of this."

"Do you need help?"

He shook his head. "I can handle this myself. Now, go."

Mabel lingered for a moment. Then he kissed her on the cheek.

"Please, go," he said. "It's for your own good."

Mabel took his hand and held onto it as she pulled away, eventually letting go and returning to the dance. The orchestra broke into another fox trot, but Richard, for once in his life, wasn't even interested. If Yutaka had somehow survived that fall into the river and purchased a ticket for the President Madison, Richard realized this wasn't about the assignment anymore. Yutaka wanted retribution.

And Richard wanted off the ship.

He found the stairwell and ascended two flights to the top deck where he could see Yutaka coming. With most of the passengers either in the ballroom or lower decks, Richard found the area to be perfect for inviting a showdown. Four exits—one on each side of the boat—and the bridge just above them gave Richard escape hatches as well as witnesses to anything Yutaka wanted to do.

But Richard needed Yutaka to find his way to the top.

Richard found a newspaper, an edition of The Seattle Times from three weeks earlier, and started reading it while reclining on a bench. And he waited.

An hour passed and Richard didn't see another soul as he read by the dim lights strung overhead. He started to wonder if his mind was playing tricks on him and he hadn't really seen Yutaka.

But Richard suddenly felt Yutaka's presence—along with his cold, sharp dagger.

CHAPTER 25

RICHARD FROZE, ANTICIPATING THE POINT JABBING THE base of his neck ripping through his skin. He swallowed hard and waited for Yutaka to speak. After a long, uncomfortable pause, Richard decided to say something.

"If you're going to do it, why haven't you done it already?" Richard asked.

"A samurai always waits until the moment is right," Yutaka said.

"You were a samurai?"

"It might be difficult to believe, but it's true. It was a very long time ago."

"When is the moment going to be right?"

"Right after you tell me where the cipher is?"

Richard slowly shook his head. "I don't have any ciphers."

"Did you give them to your friends at the consulate?"

"Would you believe me if I told you that I didn't?"

Yutaka drew in a deep breath then exhaled slowly. "Probably not."

"Then what difference does it make what I tell you?"

"Before I kill you, I will at least allow you to die with dignity and honor," Yutaka said. "There is a scenario where you can escape this situation alive."

Richard's eyes widened. "And what scenario is that?"

"The one where you give me the cipher and we never speak again."

"There's just one problem with that," Richard said. "I don't have a cipher to give you."

Three . . . two . . . one . . .

Richard dove onto the ground and rolled for a few yards before bouncing back up to his feet. He was now facing Yutaka who'd hurdled the bench and had edged closer to Richard while waving a knife at him. Richard was surprised at how agile the big man was.

"I don't know what you're trying to prove," Richard said. "Are you still offended about how we left things on the train to Chosi? I promise it wasn't anything personal."

"It won't be personal when I throw you overboard and loot your room for the cipher," Yutaka said. "It'll just be business."

"Before you do any of that, you'll have to catch me."

Richard feigned to his left for a second before breaking right and dashing across the deck. Yutaka took a swipe at Richard but missed widely.

"Do you think you'll be able to avoid me forever?" Yutaka asked.

Richard danced on the balls of his feet, thinking of a reply as he plotted his next move. "Not if you stalk me in ballrooms like that. Eventually people are going to think you want to do the foxtrot with me."

"You're not as nimble as you think," Yutaka said before charging at Richard.

Richard waited as long as he could before dashing to the starboard side of the deck. Yutaka failed to connect, this time stumbling as he jabbed.

Yutaka regained his footing and then stormed around

the deck, growling and muttering something in Japanese. Richard sought an opening through which to gain the upper hand on Yutaka. Then an idea came to mind, and Richard quickly changed his tactics.

"Okay, you're right," Richard said. "I do have a cipher. And there's only one way you're going to get it—over my dead body. So come and get it."

Yutaka glared at Richard before making another run at him.

Richard stood pat against the railing as he fingered the loose end of a rope that was tied to a lifeboat suspended above the deck. The moment Yutaka drew close enough, Richard held tight to the cord and jumped over the side. He swung below, intending to return to the deck with a weapon—and the captain. But in an instant, that plan changed.

"Richard, are you up here?" a woman called from the third deck.

"Mabel, no," Richard shouted. "Go back to the ballroom."

Seconds later, he heard her scream followed by Yutaka's laugh. "New deal, Mr. Halliburton. Bring me the cipher now or the girl dies."

Richard scrambled up the rope to the top deck and found Yutaka holding Mabel, his knife to her throat.

"You have two minutes to bring it to me or else your little friend here is going to take a late night plunge into the ocean," Yutaka said. "Do you understand?"

Richard nodded and darted toward the stairwell. With Mabel dragged into the standoff, he needed to give Yutaka something to let her go. But the pressing question was what. Richard certainly wasn't about to part willingly with the cipher. He needed to improvise.

Richard hustled past the dining room, where the ship's staff were already preparing tables for the meal in the morning. He spotted a line of wooden pepper grinders and slipped inside to take one. Rushing back to the top deck, he found a small crowd had gathered, all pleading with Yutaka to release Mabel. Among the group was the captain.

"If you don't release her this instant, you'll be dealt with severely upon arriving at port," the captain said.

"I don't care about reaching port."

"Then what do you care about?" the captain asked.

Yutaka nodded at Richard. "Ask him."

The captain shot a glance at Richard, who held his hand up. "I'll handle this."

With the deck lighting so dim, Richard was betting that Yutaka would fall for the ruse, at least long enough to release Mabel. He held up the object.

"Is this what you're looking for?" Richard asked.

Yutaka grunted. "I need to inspect it first."

Richard shook his head. "You let Mabel go first."

"Not until I see the cipher."

Richard walked to the center of the deck and placed the object on the ground. "Come see for yourself."

Yutaka grabbed some nearby rope and used it to quickly secure his hostage to the railing. Then he strode to the middle before kneeling and picking up the pepper grinder.

"Do you think this is funny?" Yutaka asked. "This isn't a cipher."

"That's the genius of it," Richard said. "It's a functioning pepper grinder but also serves as a cipher."

"Your attempts to take me for an idiot will cost your friend her life."

He spun and marched toward Mabel, turning his back on Richard and the other onlookers. Richard didn't hesitate, breaking into a sprint to catch Yutaka. Mabel screamed, pleading for Yutaka to spare her life. But he didn't break his stride.

Richard closed in on Yutaka, who spun around and was bracing for impact and clutching his dagger.

At the moment before collision, Richard slid feet first, catching Yutaka by surprise. The resulting contact knocked him to the ground, sending him tumbling several feet before coming to rest against the railing. Richard jumped up and worked furiously to free Mabel.

Yutaka growled as he staggered to his feet, just in time to watch his hostage run across the deck to join the crowd, which had doubled since Richard's return from the dining room.

"You think you're going to get away with this?" Richard asked.

Yutaka narrowed his eyes. "Give me the cipher."

"You're never going to get it because I don't have it."

"Your lies are getting tiresome."

"Not nearly as much as your pursuit of something that doesn't exist on this ship."

Richard eyed Yutaka as he paced around the deck.

"I'm going to kill you," he said with a growl.

"And you'll still have no cipher. You'll just be a murderer, shamed for being unable to complete your assignment, a mission that was always going to fail because I never took a cipher."

Yutaka let out an exasperated breath before suddenly turning toward Richard and charging him. However, Richard had been moving slowly to place his back against the railing, getting in just the right position. As Yutaka closed in, he drew his knife back and prepared to thrust it into Richard. But just as the blade was on a course for Richard's chest, he dropped to the deck before exploding upward, catching Yutaka in the waist and bending him over.

Richard yelled as he muscled the Japanese man off the floor and over the railing. Yutaka screamed as he fell, flailing into the ocean and splashing down. The crowd rushed over to see what had happened. One man shouted about a passenger being overboard, but the captain held up his hand.

"Justice has been served," the captain said. "We won't attempt to rescue him."

Richard nodded knowingly at the captain.

Mabel rushed over and nearly tackled Richard with a hug. "Thank you. I've never been more scared in my life."

"Me either," he said.

As the crowd dispersed, the captain grabbed Richard by the arm. "We need to talk."

CHAPTER 26

Seattle, Washington

WHEN RICHARD ARRIVED IN SEATTLE, HE TOOK A deep breath as he stepped onto the ramp. After all the time he'd spent at sea, he could hardly smell the salty air swirling around him. He took off his winter coat, tucking it underneath his arm, happy to bask in Seattle's mild temperatures.

The customs agent eyed Richard as he approached the kiosk. "Sir, it's a bit chilly outside. You might want to put that back on when you leave."

Richard placed his document on the counter. "If I could get away with taking my shirt off, I would. You have no idea how cold I've been for the past few months."

The man shrugged. "To each his own, I guess," he said as he scanned the papers. He handed them back to Richard and directed him where to go. However, Richard never reached the door.

Hank Foster blocked the way.

"You sure do get around," he said, a wide grin spreading across his face. "Come with me," Foster said. "We have much to discuss."

Foster led Richard to a car waiting outside. The driver hopped out of the front and opened the trunk for Richard, helping him with his luggage. Once they were all inside,

Foster directed the man to take them to the U.S. Army's intelligence offices overlooking the Puget Sound.

Richard rubbed his hands together as he stared out the window. He was relieved to be home after nearly getting murdered on the President Madison, but he also held Foster suspect after using strong-arm tactics to get Richard to go along with the cipher mission in Japan.

"So, did you get it?" Foster asked in a hushed tone.

Richard nodded, keeping his gaze locked on the passing scenery outside.

"That's great news. I was a little worried after I heard that you ran into some trouble."

Richard forced a laugh. "Trouble? That's what you call getting hunted by the Kenpetai?"

"There are other words I could use for it, I guess," Foster said. "I just realize what you did wasn't easy."

"No, it wasn't," Richard snapped.

Foster grabbed Richard's arm and tugged on it. Richard turned to find Foster with his head cocked to one side.

"Are you all right?" Foster asked.

Richard ripped his arm away from the Army Intelligence officer. "I'm fine."

"You look about like my wife does when she tells me she's fine. And I know it's all a big lie."

"I'm beginning to wonder if the big lie was you saying you would help me secure a publisher if I did what you asked," Richard said. "Which I've done, by the way."

"I'm sorry if you felt I was manipulating you," Foster said. "We really needed your assistance in the matter."

"And how many more times are you going to need my assistance before you actually give me all the contact information you promised you would? Ten? Fifteen? Twenty? Fifty? A hundred? This is a slippery slope, Foster, and you know it."

"I know how this must look to you, but in our business, you oftentimes have small windows to secure pertinent information. And if you don't do it, it could cost the lives of very good people who would be unsuspectingly thrown into harm's way. Do you want that to happen?"

Richard shook his head. "There you go again."

"Go again? What are you talking about?"

"You're trying to manipulate me with this story of yours, a blatant attempt to play on my sympathies to get me to do what you want."

"I'm simply explaining why I did what I did."

"And you're about to ask me to do something else for you, aren't you?"

Foster remained quiet. He took a deep breath and then put his hands on his knees. It was his turn to stare outside the window and brood.

After a few minutes, Richard broke the awkward silence. "You know I love my country, don't you?"

Foster managed a slight nod.

"So just ask me next time. Don't try to hold something over my head. Keep your word and shoot me straight. We'll get along famously if you'll remember those things."

"I think I can do that," Foster said before reaching into his pocket and handing Richard an envelope. "This is yours. You've earned it."

Richard opened it up and scanned the letter from William Feakins, president of the Feakins Agency. Mr. Feakins stated that he would be interested in meeting to discuss the terms of a deal to schedule Richard to speak about his worldwide travel. He also said with fiction sales flagging, his publisher friend at Bobbs-Merrill recently told him that the company would be going in a new direction toward non-fiction books. And according to the letter, the tales of Richard's exploits were just what the company was looking for.

He smiled as he looked up at Foster. "Is this real?"

Foster nodded. "In fact, I didn't even really have to call on any favors to get it done. Mr. Feakins has been a friend of the military's for a long time. And before I'd even finished telling him about you, he was inquiring about where he could view some of your work. Less than a week after I first spoke with him, I received a call that he was interested and would be sending me that letter."

Richard was unable to remove the grin on his face. "You have no idea how happy this makes me. I was either going to be helping my father sell real estate or slumming at a newspaper somewhere while writing obituaries. I'm quite sure either one of those would've sucked the life right out of me."

When they arrived at the office, Richard handed over the film for development while he debriefed Foster on what happened in Japan and Yutaka's attempted assassination. The fact that the Japanese tried to kill Richard angered Foster, who said he'd be speaking with his liaison at the White House about it. After they finished, an officer handed Foster a folder.

"The pictures you requested, sir," the man said.

Foster flipped through the images before ordering the man to return. "Get these to the cryptology department and have them compare that with the cable we intercepted yesterday."

Richard furrowed his brow. "You think they've already deployed these ciphers?"

Foster nodded. "Even though we lost the old cipher, we started noticing a couple of days ago that the notes had a different rhythm to them. Something changed, and we believe it started with the launch of a new decoding system."

* * *

THE NEXT MORNING, Richard made one final visit to the Army Intelligence offices to speak with Foster. When Richard walked into the building, he immediately noticed the lines creasing Foster's forehead.

"What is it?" Richard asked.

"Come with me to my office," Foster said. "We need to talk right away."

Richard waited until Foster shut the door. "What is it?"

Foster gestured toward the chair across from his desk. "Have a seat."

"Is everything all right?" Richard asked as he leaned forward.

"First of all, I can't begin to tell you how valuable the fruit of your mission was in obtaining those pictures of the cipher," Foster began. "Last night, our team here was able to build a similar one and started decoding some of the messages."

"And?"

"We've suspected that there's a Japanese agent in San Francisco who's been funneling secrets back to Tokyo for the past year or so. Now we know who he is."

"What's that got to do with me?" Richard asked.

Foster handed Richard a folder. "The person who's been passing along this information is someone you might know, a Miss Mabel Johnson."

"Mabel Johnson? I know several women named Mabel."

"This one was on your voyage from Tokyo to Seattle. She is a telegraph operator at one of our units in San Francisco, working directly for the commander of that outfit."

"Mabel, the woman whose life I saved on the ship?"

Foster shrugged. "In light of what we know now about her, I doubt her life was ever in danger."

Richard clenched his jaw as he slowly shook his head. "She was playing me the whole time. She actually pointed out that Yutaka was watching me. I should've known."

"Don't get too down on yourself," Foster said. "It happens to the best of us. Just be glad it wasn't the kind of mistake that cost you your life."

"What do you want me to do?" Richard asked.

"I know I told you getting that cipher was your last assignment," Foster said, "so, you don't have to do anything. I just—"

"You said it was the last assignment you were giving me, but I never said it was the last mission I'd take. Tell me what you want me to do because I'll do whatever you ask."

Foster leaned forward, handing Richard another stack of documents. "Here's the briefing. But in short, we want you to earn her trust so she can help you capture the Japanese spy."

"Sounds easy enough."

"Don't be so sure. She's trained in interrogation techniques and knows how to resist. You're going to have to work hard to get her to trust you, but if you can do it, it'll help us secure our dissemination chain."

"Whatever it takes."

CHAPTER 27

One week later
San Francisco, California

RICHARD HUSTLED UP THE STEPS OF THE ST. FRANCIS Hotel and strolled through the lobby. After a quick scan of the room, he went over to the elevator and stepped inside.

The employee operating it was dressed in a dark-blue suit with a maroon bowtie, his silver hair leaking beneath his cap.

"What floor, sir?" he asked.

"I'm here for the splendor," Richard said.

The man smiled and winked as he pushed a button. Moments later they were drifting downward. When they reached the basement, the doors slid open, revealing a grand party, complete with a stocked bar and a lively orchestra. Couples whirled around the dance floor, while the city's more prominent citizens chatted at the bar over drinks that were supposedly prohibited.

Richard took his hat off and soaked in the scene. He didn't move from his spot for about a minute before an unsuspected slap in the back made him stumble forward.

"Don't look so scared, kid," an elderly man said. "The mayor is here drinking with us."

Richard wasn't sure what the man meant. He pointed

toward the far corner, where a balding man in a suit and tie laughed heartily while pouring another round of shots from his bottle for the trio of men seated at his table.

"That's Mayor Rolph?" Richard asked.

"Sunny Jim himself," the man said. "Relax. You've got nothing to worry about."

Richard found an empty seat on the corner and ordered a gin and tonic. He engaged in some small talk with the man on the adjacent stool before starting to look in earnest for Mabel. Another half-hour passed before he checked his watch and glanced at the front door. He shifted his weight on the stool and ordered another drink.

According to the intelligence briefing Richard received, Mabel visited the St. Francis Hotel speakeasy every other Thursday when she wasn't away on official Army business. She allegedly slipped a treasure trove of information to her Japanese spy at this location. However, that was merely speculation as the officers assigned to determine who she was passing the intel to couldn't determine anything definitively.

Richard took a walk around the ballroom, keeping an eye out for Mabel. At a stroke before 8:00 p.m., she finally darkened the doors of the hidden establishment.

She checked her coat and then said hello to a few acquaintances before making her way to the bar.

"Mabel? Is that you?" Richard asked, feigning surprise at her appearance.

"Richard Halliburton, as I live and breathe," she said as she threw her arms around him and gave him a big hug.

She patted one of the gentlemen at the bar on the back. He turned around, and his demeanor instantly transformed once he locked eyes with Mabel.

"Christopher, I want you to meet the man who saved my life on my most recent trip," she said.

THE QUEST FOR THE FUJI CIPHER | 199

The man offered his hand to Richard. "I understand you're a real American hero."

Richard shrugged. "Just doing what any man would do in a situation like that."

Christopher chuckled and shook his head. "I'd let Mabel twist in the wind because then I could dance without getting my toes stepped on."

Mabel swatted him playfully with her clutch. "Watch yourself or else you might end up dancing all alone in the corner like a deranged lunatic."

"Who's crazier? The man who dances alone to save his toes? Or the man who allows his feet to get trampled by elephant foot over there?"

Mabel shoved him gently in the back. "Maybe it's not me. Maybe it's my partner."

The crowd of drinkers nearby had been joining the back-and-forth conversation, drawing "oohs" with every biting comment.

"She might have a point, sir," Richard said. "I didn't have any issues when we were partners."

Christopher rolled his eyes and waved dismissively at Richard. "Look everybody, the white knight has arrived, here to save the damsel in distress."

Richard was about to lecture the man on how to treat a lady when Mabel put her index finger to his lips with one hand and pulled him aside with the other.

"It's not worth it," she said. "Just leave him alone."

Richard glanced over his shoulder at Christopher, giving him a knowing look. She saw Richard staring back at the bar before gently turning his jaw so he was facing her.

"Look here," she said. "Forget about him."

"Nobody should treat a lady like that."

"No gentleman should treat anyone like that," she

corrected. "But like all of us, he has his moments where he forgets who he is."

"I suppose," Richard admitted.

"So, what are you doing in San Francisco? I'm still in shock that you're here."

"Just wanted to make a few stops while I was out west before returning home to Memphis. I've got to start writing my book."

"Of course you do," she said. "Seems to me that you'd rather just travel around."

"That sounds simply sublime. But since I'm not independently wealthy, I'm required to actually do some work."

"So is tonight work or pleasure?"

"A mixture of both."

She placed her drink on a nearby table and encouraged him to do the same. "Why don't we engage in a little bit of pleasure? I just heard the band leader announce that a fox trot is coming up next."

"Why not," Richard said with a warm smile.

Moments later, they were on the dance floor, moving back and forth to the rhythms of the smooth melody. When the song was finished, a waltz followed. She drew Richard close and gazed into his eyes.

"Tell me why you're really here, Richard," she said. "And please tell me what I want to hear."

"I'm not sure what you want to hear," he said.

"Oh, I think you do. That night on the President Madison when that Japanese spy attacked me—you can't deny there wasn't a connection."

"Maybe," Richard said. "But I'm not here for any connection we made. I'm here for a connection that you make every other week here at the St. Francis Hotel."

She stopped dancing and pulled back. "What are you talking about?"

"You know exactly what I'm talking about.."

"I thought you were here to see me."

"I am, but not for the reason you think. As soon as I arrived in Seattle, I was briefed by Army Intelligence about the kind of operation you're running."

"I haven't the slightest idea about what you're referring to."

"Passing government secrets on to Japanese spies, men like Yutaka."

"I never met him before in my life."

"Unfortunately, I'd be a fool to believe that. Now, where is the man you pass your information off to?"

"That's not why I come here."

"Don't play games with me," Richard said. "All we have to do is leak that you're a suspected traitor and you'd be ruined—or maybe dead in a couple of days."

"You wouldn't dare," she said as she narrowed her eyes.

"It's your life. Is this something you want to gamble with?"

"How could you turn so cold?" she said as a tear trickled down her cheek. "I thought we had a connection on the ship."

"I thought you were in real danger. I guess we were both wrong. Now, what's the protocol for passing off the information to your contact?"

She set her jaw. "Just don't."

"Nobody made you do this."

"You don't know why I did this, do you? Do you?"

Richard shrugged. "Your motives aren't my concern. Keeping our country safe is."

"It's my mother," Mabel said, plowing ahead with her explanation. "She's sick and dying. And the only way I could afford to pay the medical bills was to get another job. But the Army won't let me do anything else other than what I'm doing. And I couldn't just let her die."

"You could get a different job."

"Do you know how difficult it is for a woman to make ends meet on her own in this world?"

Richard sighed. "I sympathize with your plight, but there are other ways to deal with a situation like this that don't include becoming a traitor."

"I don't want your sympathy."

"What do you want then?"

"I want you to turn around and walk out of here, pretend like you never saw me. Tell whoever it is you answer to that they were wrong about me."

Richard shook his head. "That's not going to happen."

Mabel slipped her hand into her purse and pulled out a small pistol. "Oh, it isn't?"

"Mabel, you're going down the wrong path. You know you're not going to shoot me. Put down your gun and do the right thing."

She glared at him. "I am doing the right thing."

Then she cut her eyes over at Christopher, who hopped off his stool and started walking toward Richard. She gave him a subtle head shake, but Richard noticed it.

"He's your contact?" Richard asked.

"No, he's just a friend," she said, her voice quivering.

"I don't believe you. Prove me wrong."

"He's not even Japanese. How could he be my contact?"

"I'm guessing he's a dock worker and would be the perfect liaison for you to pass your messages through. Nobody would suspect a thing. Until now."

"You're wrong. That's not him. He's not my contact.

He doesn't even work at the docks."

Christopher drew nearer, his gaze bouncing between Richard and Mabel.

"Lower your gun before somebody gets hurt," Richard said. "Nobody needs to die tonight."

Christopher froze when he noticed Mabel's gun. "Is everything all right over here?"

"We were just talking about you," Richard said. "How you love working on the docks and managing all your crews."

"I'm not sure I believe that's what you were talking about," Christopher said as he clenched his fists.

"Are you looking for a fight?" Richard asked.

"No, but maybe you are," Christopher sneered.

"Mabel here was just telling me that you're the one she's handing off all her intelligence secrets to. And I'm here to arrest you both."

Christopher eyed Richard and Mabel for a beat before dashing toward the exit. With the elevator unavailable, Christopher swerved and raced toward the stairwell. Richard remained right behind him, while Mabel tried to keep up.

The temporary chaos drew gasps from the other drinkers in the speakeasy. But the noise never rose above the level of mild curiosity as no one followed them.

Richard managed to keep pace with Christopher, remaining only five or six strides behind. When they reached street level, Christopher broke to the right, shoving his way past one hotel guest who expressed his displeasure with the rude behavior.

They both rounded the corner, charging hard into an alley. Richard's sides burned as he maintained the blistering speed at which Christopher was running. Meanwhile, Mabel didn't lag too far behind.

Christopher turned a corner only to stop in his tracks.

As Richard reached the intersection, a truck was facing them, filling the narrow passageway. Christopher was trapped.

A few seconds later, Richard turned around to see Mabel walking toward them, her gun trained in front of her.

"Look, Mabel, you don't have to do this," Richard said. "If you cooperate, I'm sure the Army will go easy on you."

"No, Mabel, they won't," Christopher countered. "Shoot him, and let's get out of here. Our plan is solid. We can disappear in a matter of hours."

Mabel held her gun on Richard. "They won't go easy on me," she said. "You're just doing whatever it takes to save yourself."

Then Mabel moved her aim toward Christopher and pulled the trigger. He collapsed on the ground, his chest bleeding profusely.

"And so am I," she said as she walked over to Christopher as he gasped for air.

Mabel handed the gun to Richard. "Take me in. Do whatever you need to do, but this is over for me tonight, one way or another."

Richard pocketed the weapon and then rushed onto the street. He grabbed a passerby and asked them to call the police.

"There's been a shooting."

CHAPTER 28

February 29, 1923
Memphis, Tennessee

RICHARD STARED OUT THE WINDOW AT HIS FATHER'S pickup truck as they bumped along the road to his first scheduled lecture at West Tennessee State. Tales of his escapades across three continents drew so much interest that he asked the college to host him so he could go anywhere in town without getting bombarded with questions.

"Nervous?" Wesley Halliburton asked.

Richard shook his head.

"You sure are quiet."

"Just thinking," Richard said.

"About what?"

"About everything, even Wesley Jr."

Richard attempted to manage the emotions flooding his mind. He was excited about getting to test out his subject material, viewing his lecture as a trial run about what to put in his book and what to leave out based on the audience's reaction. And he also experienced a deep sadness that his little brother couldn't be here to witness the moment. But if Wesley Jr. had been still been alive, Richard wasn't sure he would've ever taken the leap. He'd probably be in graduate school somewhere, piling on another boring degree as his life dwindled away in front of his eyes.

Then there was what to make of his adventures working for Hank Foster and the U.S. Army Intelligence, absolutely enthralling stories he could never talk about publicly—or privately, for that matter. They were thrilling and monumental in some ways. Had it not been for his dogged determination to go toe to toe with Germans and the Japanese, the world he lived in might be very different.

However, he couldn't stop thinking about Mabel and if he did the right thing. Richard knew she was a traitor, but was she really? Or was she just a confused woman trying to help her ailing mother?

After he told the police what happened, Richard had convinced them that Mabel was a hero. But he wasn't sure that was the same story he wanted to tell Foster. The police allowed Mabel to go free that night, but Richard didn't. He wanted to know the truth. Was her mother really sick?

Mabel had taken him to St. Mary's Hospital where her mother was fighting for her life in a hospital bed. She'd been diagnosed with a degenerative condition in her spine that incapacitated her and required constant monitoring that could only happen in a hospital. The bills mounted quickly. And Mabel did was she could, not because she hated her country but because she loved her mother.

In the end, Mabel's reason did matter to Richard. Convinced that she was acting only out of fear for her mother, he told Foster that Christopher, the real spy who had approached Mabel, was about to kill him, but Mabel saved Richard's life. She gunned Christopher down as he was about to kill Richard.

Richard convinced Foster to give Mabel a raise and to find assistance for her mother. Mabel was transferred to another office in Seattle, along with her mother. Mabel had sent a telegram to Richard, expressing her displeasure at the move. But she begrudgingly admitted that it was better than prison. She also thanked him for getting help for her mother.

Richard remained lost in thought for a few more minutes before Wesley pulled into the main parking lot. After he turned off the truck, Richard broke his silence.

"Does it ever get any easier, Dad?" he asked.

"Does what get any easier?"

"Life."

"Life is a beautiful tapestry of joy and pain," Wesley said. "Without each other, we wouldn't appreciate those shining moments where everything comes together."

"But what if it never does?"

"Then we keep trying. Our lives aren't about what we accomplish. Instead, they're about the journeys we take when we try."

Richard nodded. "When did you get to be so wise?"

Wesley chuckled. "I haven't traveled the world like you have, son, but there are plenty of miles under this old hood."

Richard checked his watch and gasped. "I gotta go or else I'll be late."

He jumped out of the truck and then sprinted up the steps of the building. Once inside, a couple school administrators greeted him and guided him to the area backstage.

"Are you ready?" one of the men asked.

"I've never done this before," Richard said. "But then again, I'd never traveled the world either until I started two years ago."

"Well, that turned out fine, didn't it?"

Richard smiled. "Here's to hoping this does too."

* * *

RICHARD FINISHED his lecture to thunderous applause. Albert Feakins stood waiting in the wings, sent to hear

Richard live to get a feel for his stage presence.

"That was fabulous," Albert said. "I'm going to tell my father to send you a contract straight away."

A wide grin spread across Richard's face. "Are you serious?"

Albert nodded. "I wouldn't lie to you about something like this. Now don't hold me to this, but I'll be shocked if my father can't get Bobbs-Merrill excited about a book on this same subject. He and William Bobbs are golfing buddies."

"The William Bobbs?"

Albert nodded. "They play once a month at different clubs around New York."

"You better not be fooling with me," Richard said, wagging his finger.

"One day you're going to be a bigger name than my father or even William Bobbs," Albert said. "That much you can bank on."

"You're too kind," Richard said.

Albert apologized that he needed to run, but he had another meeting to get to.

Richard shook some of the students' hands before meandering out of the building. When he got back to his dad's truck, Hank Foster was leaning against it.

"Great speech, Richard," Foster said. "I almost believed half of it."

"That's because I only told half of the truth," Richard said with a chuckle. "If I told them everything, they would call me a liar and boo me off the stage."

"I don't doubt that."

"Where's my dad?" Richard asked.

"I sent him to go get a cup of coffee."

"Why are you here? What's going on?"

Foster stroked his chin. "I won't beat around the bush.

We need you, Richard."

"That's flattering, but I think you just saw in there that I have my sights set on other goals."

"I understand—and I'm not asking you to change that. I'm just hoping you'd be willing to work for us on a more permanent basis while you continue to do whatever it is you plan to do on your world travels. President Harding has heard about you and—"

"Wait. Did you say President Harding?"

Foster nodded.

"He knows who I am?"

"Everyone in Washington is starting to talk about the boy wonder intelligence officer."

"That's flattering, but I want you to understand that writing and traveling and exploring—those are my passions, not spying."

"I understand. Does that mean you're saying no?"

Richard stared off in the distance before returning his gaze to Foster. "I wouldn't have half the adventures I've had without you. And let's be honest, looking at incredible monuments and natural scenery will probably get boring after a while."

Foster's eyes brightened. "So you'll do it?"

"Count me in," Richard said.

"In that case," Foster said as a wide smile spread across his lips, "there's something I need to talk to you about."

Richard shrugged. "Of course there is. Let's hear it."

EPILOGUE

June 5, 1932

RICHARD ENTERED HIS PARENTS' HOME, THE SCREEN door clattering shut behind him. He glided through the kitchen and found a basket full of letters. Responding to letters was something he used to enjoy, but the amount of fan mail he received as his popularity grew made the task a tiresome one.

However, as he was flipping through the letters, there was one postmarked location that caught his eye: Tokyo, Japan. He ripped open the envelope and started reading:

Dear Richard,

I've been meaning to write you but never knew how to reach you—until now. I was recently in a bookshop and saw your book, The Royal Road to Romance, translated into Japanese. It was as wonderful as I imagined. However, I must say that your summit of Mt. Fuji was quite boring compared to what actually happened.

I also wanted to let you know that Thomas Lees and I eventually married and have had a wonderful life together. Every time I see my husband's rugged face, I can't help

but think how you brought us together. And
for that, I am forever grateful.
Signed,
Hisako Hoya-Lees

P.S. I told you that you'd be famous one day.

Richard smiled and set the letter aside. He would
definitely respond to it sooner rather than later.

THE END

Acknowledgments

This project has been incredibly exciting and fun to embark upon, mixing fiction with fact. And quite frankly, none of it would've ever come about without my wife's introduction of Richard Halliburton to me through his timeless Book of Marvels. My children also played a huge role in convincing me to write something about Halliburton after they read his books and would regale me with his stories everyday until I finally decided I needed to read them for myself.

I'd like to thank Rhodes College and Bill Short for allowing me access to Richard Halliburton's archived journals and other material that helped fill in the blanks about what kind of man Richard really was and where he really went. Bill was an incredible help in gathering the information for me and graciously allowing me to plod my way through the material I requested. Without Bill's assistance, I'm not sure this project would've ever become a reality—at least in my lifetime.

Sir Richard J. Evans also enthusiastically aided the creation of this story in giving me plausible creative ways to weave the storyline of the Reichswehr into this fictionalized tale. I'm so grateful that when I reached out to him that he was more than gracious in supplying me with ample fodder— material that will be used in future novels in this series.

And as always, this book wouldn't be what it is without Krystal Wade's skillful editorial direction. She made this book much better than when I originally conceived it.

John Pirhalla has been incredible to partner with in creating the audio version of this book, and I look forward to his voice being the one that shares many more Richard Halliburton tales in the future.

And last but certainly not least, I'm most grateful for you, the reader, who decided to invest your time with one of my stories. I hope you had as much fun reading this book as I did writing it.

MORE RICHARD HALLIBURTON ADVENTURES

The Secret of the King's Tomb
The Raja's Last Treasure
The Hidden Seal of the Realm
The Quest for the Fuji Cipher
The Chase for the General's Gold

Made in the USA
Coppell, TX
22 December 2023

26814444R00127